mary-kateandashley
so little time

Check out these other great
so little time
titles:

Book 1: **how to train a boy**

Book 2: **instant boyfriend**

Book 3: **too good to be true**

Book 4: **just between us**

Book 5: **tell me about it**

Book 6: **secret crush**

Book 7: **girl talk**

Book 8: **the love factor**

Book 9: **dating game**

Coming soon!

Book 10: **a girl's guide to guys**

mary-kateandashley
so little time
dating game

by Kylie Adams

Based on the teleplay by Becky Southwell

📖 HarperCollins*Entertainment*
An Imprint of HarperCollins*Publishers*

A PARACHUTE PRESS BOOK

A PARACHUTE PRESS BOOK

Parachute Publishing, L.L.C.
156 Fifth Avenue
Suite 325
NEW YORK
NY 10010

First published in the USA by HarperEntertainment 2003
First published in Great Britain by HarperCollins*Entertainment* 2003
HarperCollins*Entertainment* is an imprint of HarperCollins*Publishers* Ltd,
77-85 Fulham Palace Road, Hammersmith, London W6 8JB

The HarperCollins website address is
www.harpercollins.co.uk

1 3 5 7 9 10 8 6 4 2

ISBN 0 00 714454 7

Printed and bound in Great Britain by Clays Ltd, St Ives plc

chapter
one

"**S**top! That is so gross!" Riley Carlson cried.

Fourteen-year-old Chloe Carlson hushed her twin sister. "No, wait," she insisted. "You have to hear this part, too." Trying hard not to laugh, she read aloud from the school newspaper: "'There is so much grease on the pizza served in West Malibu High's cafeteria that it hovers over each slice like smog.'" Chloe closed the paper and shook her head. "I would love to trade places with this kid. The biggest problem he can come up with for the 'Sound Off' column is greasy pizza. Hello? There are other issues in the world. Doesn't he watch *Entertainment Tonight*?"

Riley groaned. "You know, I might write a 'Sound Off' myself."

Chloe checked her watch and relaxed. There were still a few minutes to spare before homeroom started. "Really? About what?"

"For starters, the boring assignments I get stuck

with for that paper," Riley said.

"Well, you *did* sign up in the middle of the semester. Instead of a staff writer, you're a floater. I guess that's kind of like being an intern at a big company. You know, boring, no glory, no perks…"

Riley raised her hand. "Enough – I get the point."

Chloe smiled. "But there was that story you did on the new coffee machine in the teachers' lounge. You know, that was really exciting. It should've been a two-parter." She laughed.

Riley pursed her lips.

Uh-oh, Chloe thought. Maybe I took the teasing a step too far. "You know I'm kidding, right?" she asked, giving her sister a friendly shove.

"Well, you shouldn't really talk about my skills as a journalist," Riley admitted. "What have *you* written lately?"

"Do I have to remind you how many e-mails I get in a week? I'm *constantly* writing," Chloe replied with a grin.

"E-mails don't count," Riley protested. "I'm talking about real writing, like an article. Maybe *you* should do a 'Sound Off.'"

"On what – the mysterious meat loaf?" Chloe laughed at her own joke.

Riley cracked up, too. "I think we can move beyond the cafeteria. I'm sure there's a cause out there that you feel strongly about."

Something clicked in Chloe's brain. How could

she have forgotten? "Actually, now that you mention it, the plight of endangered sea mammals is something I'm *very* passionate about."

"Since when?" Riley asked.

"Since Mom told me that we could take boys to this year's Save the Seals benefit," Chloe replied. Save the Seals was a fancy charity dance that was tons of fun. The Carlson family attended it every year.

Riley grabbed Chloe's jacket sleeve. "Are you serious?" she asked.

Chloe nodded. "Yes, and it's this Saturday, so we have to work fast."

"*Saturday*?" A look of panic swept across Riley's face. "But it's Monday!" She paused. "Wait a minute. This would make a great first date with Vance."

Chloe had known that was coming. Vance Kohan was the cute boy Riley had met at a surf clinic. They weren't exactly dating, but as far as Chloe was concerned, they should have been.

"Vance surfs in the ocean," Riley went on. "Seals *swim* in the ocean. What could be more perfect?"

"If Freddie Prinze were single – that would be more perfect," Tara Jordan said, joining them.

Chloe laughed at Tara's one-liner. The girl was hysterical. And she was looking very state of the trend in her low-rise jeans and vintage rock tee.

Right beside her was Quinn Reyes. They were two of Chloe's closest friends.

"By the way, what are we talking about?" Quinn

asked just as Ms. Raffin passed by.

Ms. Raffin was an English teacher and the faculty sponsor for the student newspaper. "Let's not dawdle, girls," she said. "You'll be late for homeroom."

Riley managed a quick wave and made a speedy departure.

As Chloe, Tara, and Quinn started off in the direction of the science wing, Chloe filled them in on Save the Seals.

"Cool," Tara chirped. "So who are you going to ask? Hold on. Let me guess. Lennon, right?"

Just hearing his name caused Chloe's heart to skip a beat. Lennon Porter was smart and funny and super-cute. But Chloe didn't want to let Tara know just how much she liked him yet. Tara was a true friend but also a big talker. One false word and everybody at school would think Chloe was madly in love with Lennon. Including Lennon.

"Maybe," she said casually. "We went out on a date two weeks ago. It was fun. I think he likes me."

"Then you should definitely ask him," Quinn said.

[Chloe: So here's where you think: Okay, Chloe's going to ask him, right? I don't think so. Granted, this is the twenty-first century, the era of female power and such. But I'm tired of always making the first move. I mean, what's wrong with a little romance? Boy asks girl. Girl says yes. Boy shows up with candy and flowers. Girl locks herself in her room and

changes her outfit at least twenty times. Yes, that's what I want – an old-fashioned date!]

Chloe felt a flutter in her stomach. "You know what?"

"Lennon's got a cute brother who's a junior but doesn't mind dating freshman girls?" Tara asked hopefully.

Chloe laughed. "Sorry. Anyway, you're the one with the cute older brother, Tara."

"I know," Quinn said, practically swooning. "Kyle is amazing."

Tara shook her head. "I don't know why all the girls go crazy over my brother. He's a six-foot-one goofball."

"You didn't let me finish!" Chloe cried. "I'm *not* asking Lennon to the dance."

"Why not?" Tara asked.

"Because I want a little romance, thank you. Why do I always have to ask out the boy? If Lennon likes me, then *he* should be the one to ask *me*. I mean, let's face it. Boys are getting lazy. Somebody has to take a stand."

"Yeah," Quinn agreed. "Way to go, sister!"

Tara glanced at Quinn and wrinkled her nose. "Whatever…*sister*."

"All I have to do is plant the seed and let him know that I want to go to the dance," Chloe announced, smiling. "But Lennon will have to do the asking."

"Well, I hope you have a green thumb, because he's heading this way," Tara said.

Chloe glanced up and saw Lennon striding down the corridor, looking exceptionally cute in way-casual baggy jeans and a T-shirt.

He made a beeline towards her. "Hey," he said. "What's up?"

"Funny you should ask that," Quinn said.

Chloe silenced Quinn with a look. "Actually something *is* up," she told Lennon. "My mom said I could take a date to the Save the Seals benefit this weekend."

Lennon nodded. "That's cool. Well, I'll talk to you later. I'd better get to class." And off he went.

Chloe just stood there for a moment. 'That's cool?' Didn't he realise that telling him about the dance was his cue to ask her out?

"That was a perfect setup, and he totally missed it," Tara said as Chloe watched Lennon disappear down the hall. "Are you sure he's in the honours programme?"

Riley could not get the old song "Surfin' USA" out of her head – probably because she and Vance had met while learning to surf.

I wonder if the band at Save the Seals will play it, she thought. Then Vance and I could dance to it. And we could make it our song!

But first she had to ask him to the benefit.

More excited than ever about her first real date with Vance, Riley scouted the crowded halls with a determined gaze. She hadn't run into him even once today, and this was a situation that definitely couldn't wait until tomorrow.

"Dude! You are so busted!"

At the sound of his voice, Riley craned her neck to see Vance goofing around with some of his buddies.

"Vance!" she called out – a little too eagerly.

Vance and his friends turned in her direction. Vance grinned right away. One of his buddies whispered something to the other, and they proceeded to crack up.

Riley went hot with embarrassment.

Vance stepped over, waving the guys off. "Don't pay any attention to them," he assured her. "They always act like morons."

Riley took a deep breath. "There's something I really wanted to—"

"Hey," Vance cut in. "Guess what? My cousin scored me a VIP ticket for the Tribal Council concert Saturday night. Isn't that cool?"

Riley knew the band. She loved their new song, "Bad Versus Beautiful," and she'd already heard about their upcoming concert at Visible Lines, a new teen club in Beverly Hills. But right now the fact that it was happening *this* Saturday night didn't seem so cool. Her spirits sank.

"What's wrong?" Vance asked. "You look like your goldfish just croaked."

Riley attempted a smile but managed only to curl

her lips into a weak grin. "There's a big Save the Seals benefit this weekend. I thought we could go together."

Vance winced. "Do you have any idea how lucky I am to be holding a VIP ticket to Tribal Council? They're, like, huge."

"Oh, I know," Riley quickly agreed. "That's too amazing to pass up." She tried to snap out of her funk. No reason to make Vance think that her world had come to a crashing halt, even though it had, at least temporarily. "I'll figure out something."

"You will have no trouble finding a date," Vance said. "Trust me on that." He shot a look back to his buddies. "Listen, I'll talk to you later. We're meeting some other guys to play basketball."

Riley watched Vance go, feeling a minor sense of panic. No doubt Chloe had made plans with Lennon. Would she be the only one without a date for Save the Seals?

Chloe spotted Lennon at his locker, loading up his backpack with textbooks. She made a quick move in his direction. Obviously he hadn't picked up on her hint earlier. She had stewed over the situation throughout the day and decided that Lennon simply wasn't a morning person and that it was better to catch him in the afternoon. Swooping in, Chloe leaned against the locker next to his.

Lennon shut his door to lock it and saw her. He smiled.

Chloe smiled back. "How was your day?"

"Better than my night will be." He pretended his backpack weighed at least one hundred pounds. "The homework they pile on is no joke."

Chloe saw her opening and went for it. "Tell me about it." She sighed. "But sometimes it doesn't seem so bad when you have something fun to look forward to at the weekend."

Lennon laughed. "It's only Monday. You're living for the weekend already?"

Chloe halted. Was this a trick question? If she said yes, she might appear desperate. "Not exactly. It's just that there's a big event on Saturday for Save the Seals, and my Mom said I could take a date, so that's the kind of thing I have to plan. You know, finding something to wear, figuring out who might want to be my date…"

Lennon said nothing and went to work on his locker combination. "I knew I'd forgotten something." He glanced at Chloe. "My Greek mythology book."

Chloe shut her mouth tight to stop herself from screaming. For a boy so responsible about homework, Lennon certainly was clueless! Would she have to hire a skywriter to fly by West Malibu High and spell it out: ATTENTION LENNON: ASK CHLOE TO THE DANCE!

She left in a minor huff. Tara, Quinn and a few other girls were waiting by their lockers around the corner.

"So did he ask you?" Tara demanded, following her down the hall.

"No!" Chloe said hotly. She spotted Riley heading their way.

"Chloe, you'll never believe this," Riley said, joining them. "Vance can't go Saturday night. He—"

"Oh, I can believe it," Chloe cut in. She picked up her step, Riley right beside her, Tara, Quinn, and the girls directly behind them. "The boys at this school are in serious need of a talking-to."

"What good will that do?" Tara asked. "The damage was done a long time ago. Maybe their mothers didn't hug them enough when they were little or something."

Chloe marched on. She shot Riley a glance. "You know what? I think I *am* going to do one of those 'Sound Off' articles. Why waste the space on complaints about pizza when there are serious issues to put on the table?"

> [Chloe: I know, I know. It's not exactly a world crisis along the lines of global warming or a peace summit. But here we are. Chloe and Riley: two girls in need of dates and two girls without them. Yikes!]

chapter
two

When Riley walked into the house with Chloe, she sensed trouble right away. The look on Manuelo's face told her something was wrong. "Are you okay?" she asked him.

Manuelo released a heavy sigh. "You know the old saying 'Don't shoot the messenger'?"

Riley nodded.

"Well," Manuelo continued, "in this case, it's don't shoot the postman. But at the very least he deserves a kick in the—"

"Manuelo!" Chloe exclaimed, cutting him off before he had a chance to say it.

"I was going to say *caboose*," he said, gesturing wildly toward the kitchen. "Ever since he delivered today's mail, those two have been..."

Riley marched directly into the kitchen to see what all the fuss was about.

Chloe followed her.

"Then how do you explain this, Macy?" their father, Jake, was asking as he waved an envelope in their mother's face. "The Save the Seals invitation is addressed to *Mr. and Mrs.* Carlson."

Riley could tell by the vague sense of victory in her mother's eyes that she was hardly stumped for an answer.

"*Obviously*," their mother began, "the mailing list has not been updated to reflect our status as a *separated* couple."

Riley felt kind of weird. Her parents hadn't really argued since before they were separated. And what was it about? A silly invitation?

[Riley: Well, I guess it makes sense that they wouldn't always see eye to eye on things. Mom and Dad are what you might call TOTAL and COMPLETE opposites. Mom is into power lunches, power workouts and power bars. And Dad's...well, Dad's not. He's into meditation and yoga and the power of relaxation. Now he's living in a trailer park near the beach. He says the simple life is helping him find his true self. Meanwhile Mom has happily taken over their fashion design business.]

Suddenly Riley experienced a feeling of dread. If Mom and Dad decided not to go, then she and Chloe would not be attending either. And Save the Seals would be so much fun. Plus, it was tradition for Mom and Dad to burn up the dance floor at the event during the disco songs.

Jake grabbed a protein bar from the pantry and shrugged his shoulders. "Let's just go together. We'll chaperon the girls. What's the big deal?"

"It *is* a big deal," Mom argued.

Chloe turned to Riley with a worried look.

"Well, if we're separated," Macy went on, "don't you think it's in the best interests of all concerned that we remain…*separate*?"

Riley leaned in to whisper to Chloe. "I've got an idea," she said. "We should help them find dates for the dance."

"Before or after *we* find dates?" Chloe whispered back. "So far nobody is picking *us* up on Saturday night."

Riley nodded in miserable agreement.

"But you may have a point," Chloe murmured under her breath. "Because if we don't find *them* dates, there will be no reason to find ourselves dates."

"I know," Riley said. "So, how should we—"

"We have the perfect solution," Chloe said out loud. Her voice rang with a great air of confidence.

Mom and Dad looked at them with interest.

"We'll find you dates for Saturday night," Chloe said.

"Uh…yeah," Riley stammered even though she wasn't quite ready for Chloe to blurt out this idea. They didn't have a plan yet.

Dad beamed at Mom, then nodded thankfully to them. "I think I'll take you up on that. Make sure she's smart and beautiful." He laughed a little.

But Mom didn't look so thrilled about the idea. She cleared her throat. "I don't need my children to help me get a date. I'll find my own escort, thank you."

Riley breathed a sigh of relief. She knew that Chloe felt it, too. Their chance to go to the dance was safe – for the moment.

Dad chomped down on the protein bar, grinning as if he didn't have a care in the world. "This is great, girls. I'd better try on my suit and make sure it still fits. See you later!" He headed out of the house.

Mom sighed and started for her office. "Girls, you might want to make a snack. I've got a conference call scheduled with a buyer overseas, so we'll be having dinner a bit later than usual."

Almost instantly Chloe opened the fridge and pulled out yogurt, strawberries, pineapple and skim milk, then reached into the cabinet for the wheat germ and raisins.

"What are you doing?" Riley asked.

"Making a smoothie," Chloe said. "Want one?"

Not feeling very hungry, Riley shook her head. "Where are we going to find a smart and beautiful woman for Dad in five days?"

Chloe shrugged. "I don't know, but wouldn't it be great if she came with two smart and cute boys for us?"

Riley giggled, in part because the idea sounded

ridiculous, but also because she had to admit, at the same time, it sounded great!

Chloe was channel surfing, listening to the radio, sipping her smoothie, and talking on the phone with Tara – all at the same time.

"I can't believe that Lennon didn't ask you to Save the Whales," Tara was saying.

"Save the Seals," Chloe corrected her.

"Whatever," Tara chirped. "Whales, seals, baby dolphins – the point is, he *didn't* ask you. And you dropped some serious hints. I mean, you were looking pretty desperate there for a minute."

Desperate? Chloe thought. Was it really that bad?

[Chloe: Here's the best part about moments like this: one day they will be over. Right now it seems so tragic. I mean, it's practically Shakespeare, or, at the very least, a really dramatic episode of *7th Heaven*. But in some not too distant future, it will barely register as a memorable event. Of course, right now I'm totally freaking out and thinking I might have to move to Iowa to escape the humiliation.]

"Are you there?" Tara asked.

"Yes, I'm here," Chloe grumbled. "I'm trying to factor the social damage. Did everyone see me throw myself at Lennon and be completely ignored? Did it look really bad?"

"No," Tara said. "It was all pretty low-key."

Call waiting sounded in Chloe's ear. "Hold on, someone's beeping in." She hit the flash button on her phone. "Hello?"

"Is this Chloe Carlson?" a female voice asked.

The woman sounded very familiar, but Chloe couldn't quite place her. "Yes, who's this?" she asked.

"It's Ms. Raffin, dear. Listen, I'm so glad that I caught you. The school paper's in a terrible bind, and we need your help."

"But Riley's the one who writes for the paper," Chloe said.

"Oh, I realise that, dear. But I couldn't help overhearing you in the hall today discussing your interest in writing a 'Sound Off.'"

On that note Chloe reached for her smoothie and took a generous sip. Ms. Raffin didn't exactly overhear as much as she eavesdropped. Sometimes she knew more about who was starting up, breaking up and making up at West Malibu High than the students themselves!

"Could you work up something by tomorrow morning?" Ms. Raffin asked.

Chloe paused to allow the smoothie to go down. It was true, she *had* said she wanted to write a "Sound Off" this afternoon, but she wasn't really serious about it. "Well, I—"

"I'm staring at empty column space where the original 'Sound Off' column should have gone," Ms.

Raffin continued. "But no matter how bad the pizza is, I can't dedicate two columns in a row to the subject. I'm so glad you're helping me out, Chloe. You're the best! Bye, dear." Then she hung up.

That was the other thing about Ms. Raffin. She had a way of not letting you say no.

Chloe sucked in a breath. Now what was she supposed to do?

Riley walked into the room. "Dinner's almost ready," she said.

Chloe couldn't imagine sitting down to eat just then. Her mind was racing a million miles a minute.

Riley's gaze zeroed in on the phone in Chloe's hand. "Who are you talking to?"

Suddenly Chloe remembered Tara on the other line and pressed the Flash button. "Tara, I'll have to call you later."

"Was that Lennon?" Tara asked.

"I wish." Chloe groaned. "I have to go. Bye." She hung up and buried her face in a pillow.

"What's wrong?" Riley asked.

Chloe removed the pillow and brought Riley up to speed on the entire Ms. Raffin incident.

Riley perched herself on the edge of the bed. "This is no big deal. The 'Sound Off' columns are short, like, maybe one page."

This news did nothing to calm Chloe. "But I have no idea what to write about, and she expects it tomorrow morning!"

Riley considered this for a moment. "I remember seeing a famous author on television, and her advice for all new writers was to write what you know."

Chloe felt the urge to push Riley off the bed. "That still doesn't tell me what to write!"

Riley gave her sister a shrewd look. "Think about what you know."

Chloe tried to concentrate, then gave up in frustration. "Ugh! I can't even think straight. This whole Lennon thing is driving me nuts. Can you believe him? I mean, when a girl tells a boy that a dance is coming up, he should take that as a hint to ask her out!"

Riley smiled. "My point exactly. Write about that."

Chloe was stunned. "Seriously?"

"Why not? It's an issue that you feel passionately about. That's what the 'Sound Off' column is there for. You know, to vent."

Chloe warmed to the idea. "You're right!" She stomped over to the desk and snatched her laptop, booting it up as soon as she returned to the bed.

"Don't get started now," Riley said. "We're about to have dinner."

Chloe was already turning on the word processing program. "Tell Mom I'm not hungry. I'll put something in the microwave later."

"Okay," Riley said.

Chloe barely noticed her sister leave the room. She was too wrapped up in her first "Sound Off." And once Lennon read it, he would know exactly what to do.

Hopefully.

chapter
three

"**R**iley!"

She spun around to see Ms. Raffin rushing toward her.

Secretly Riley wished that she hadn't been spotted. The last thing in the world she had time for was another lame newspaper assignment along the lines of new furniture for the principal's office.

"Turns out the Carlson girls are my most valuable players this week," Ms. Raffin gushed. "Chloe saved the paper last night, and now I need you—"

"Ms. Raffin," Riley began, hoping to beg off another lame assignment, "I'm completely swamped—"

"Oh, dear, please don't tell me that!" Ms. Raffin's face crashed in disappointment. "Peter Brenner is out with strep throat—"

"Wait a minute," Riley blurted out, suddenly entertaining a change of heart. "Peter Brenner? He's the sports editor."

Ms. Raffin's nod was serious. "I know, and there's a very important story on the varsity football team that has to be covered right away."

Riley's mind went into hyperdrive. The football team was full of cute boys. Granted, a footballer wasn't her first choice for a date, but one would do in a pinch.

Seemingly deep in thought, Ms. Raffin bit down on her lower lip. "But since you're so busy, I suppose I could ask—"

"I'm busy, yes," Riley interrupted, "but I'm never too busy for the school paper. At heart I'm a journalist. I realise how important it is to get the story."

Ms. Raffin beamed. "So young and already so professional. You are going to go very far, dear."

Riley was already at work thinking up an angle for the article. Maybe a profile on the cutest players without steady girlfriends. Yes! That would definitely interest West Malibu High readers. After all, a true journalist always thinks of her audience.

[Riley: I admit it. I don't really care about the West Malibu High audience. You and I both know that I have a personal interest in this story. Somewhere underneath all those helmets and protective gear is a cute boy who would love to take me to the dance!]

"Coach Lee is expecting to talk to you during your lunch period," Ms. Raffin informed her. "Bring back a hard-hitting piece about the team's new offensive line."

"Yes, hard-hitting," Riley assured her, lowering the pitch of her voice to what she hoped was a serious-and-capable tone.

All the excitement burned away Riley's appetite, but she realised that she had to eat something and gobbled up an energy bar on her way to see Coach Lee.

His office was located just off the weight centre in the gym. The door was ajar. Riley peered inside to see Coach Lee sitting at his desk, reviewing video footage from a previous game on a small television.

She observed him for a moment, then rapped on the door. "Coach Lee?"

He peered up and smiled instantly. "Are you that nosy sports reporter I've been expecting?" His tone was teasing, and his eyes crinkled with amusement.

Riley smiled and stepped inside. "Is this a bad time?"

Coach Lee reached for the remote, zapped off the TV, and spun around to face her. "You have my undivided attention." He gestured to the empty chair in front of his desk. "Have a seat."

"Thanks," Riley said, settling in and fishing through her backpack to retrieve a small notebook and pen. Coach Lee seemed approachable enough, and Ms. Raffin probably wouldn't mind her unconventional angle on the story. In fact, she just might admire Riley for going with her instincts.

Coach Lee's chair squeaked as he leaned back and folded his arms. "Fire away."

Riley was struck by Coach Lee's surroundings. A large aquarium filled with exotic fish dominated the side table, and an assortment of enormous seashells served as paperweights on his cluttered desk. Tacked on the wall was a giant picture calendar, also ocean related. This month featured seals.

What an amazing coincidence! Mom has no date for Save the Seals, and sitting before Riley is a very nice and cool man who obviously appreciates seals. Riley casually let her gaze fall on Coach Lee's hands. No wedding ring. Hmmm. Very interesting.

[Riley: Sure, Mom says that she can find her own date, but chances are she'll get caught up in work and forget all about it. I'm sitting in front of a handsome, apparently single man who obviously has a thing for the sea. It's not such a stretch to think that he would enjoy attending Save the Seals with a beautiful and successful woman. Don't you agree? Me, too.]

Riley pointed to a large seal pictured on his calendar. "Isn't it a shame about the plight of the seal? I wish everyone understood how endangered some of our sea mammals are."

Coach Lee returned a grave nod. "Some of the research is downright frightening. My grandfather was an oceanographer, so I was taught an appreciation for sea creatures early on."

"You know, there's a Save the Seals benefit this weekend," Riley said.

"I didn't know that."

"Are you a good dancer?" Riley asked.

"I can hold my own." Coach Lee gave her a quizzical look. "Do you plan on asking me any questions about the football team?"

Riley waved off the suggestion. "Oh, we'll get to that in a minute." She scooted her chair closer to Coach Lee's desk, as if letting him in on a conspiracy. "I have it on good authority that a very attractive woman about your age is holding an extra ticket to the Save the Seals benefit on Saturday night."

Coach Lee grinned. "Is that so?"

"Yes," Riley said, glancing around to make certain there were no prying eyes or ears. "Of course, this is all very confidential."

"Oh, of course," Coach Lee said.

"But if I were in your shoes, I would keep my date book open for Saturday night."

"As it happens, I'm free."

Riley couldn't believe this stroke of luck. Chloe would be thrilled.

"So, can you give me a hint? Who is this mystery woman?"

"My mom," Riley said.

Coach Lee did a double take.

"But it's a secret. She doesn't like the idea of someone helping her find a date, so when you meet her, don't let on that we've had this conversation."

"My lips are sealed," he said. "I do have one question though."

"What's that?" Riley asked.

"How are the two of us supposed to meet?" Coach Lee replied.

Riley leaned back. "Leave that to me."

"So you have a plan?" Coach Lee asked.

"Yes…well, not exactly…uh…all the particulars are still being worked out." Riley could feel her left eye twitching, which always happened when she lied. Luckily Coach Lee was not hip to this fact. He seemed to be buying her story. But Riley would definitely need Chloe's help to finish the job!

Coach Lee checked his watch. "We'd better get on with the story, Riley. Time is getting away from us."

"Oh, yes," Riley agreed. "You're absolutely right." She cleared her throat and sat up straight. "Speaking of the story, I was thinking of mixing things up and coming at this from a whole new angle."

Coach Lee gave her a strange look. "I thought this was just a simple announcement of the new offensive line."

"Well, that's probably how Peter would have approached it. But he's a boy." She paused to emphasise her point. "And I'm a girl. So instead of printing another laundry list of players and positions, why not offer our readers something different?"

Coach Lee grinned. "Such as?"

"Pictures of all the guys and their current dating status," Riley said.

Coach Lee was laughing now. "Well, that's certainly a different approach."

"I'm serious," Riley insisted. "Can you think of a better way to get girls to read the sports page? Or buy advance tickets to the games?"

Coach Lee shook a finger at her. "You just may have a point there, Riley." He stood up. "Okay, you've convinced me. Let's do it." From the top drawer of the filing cabinet he grabbed a thick brown envelope. "You're in luck. Our official team photos just came in. Every player in the starting lineup posed for an individual shot, too."

Riley dug right in and began sorting through the pictures as if they were playing cards. Wow. There was definitely something to be said for boys who played football. Drop-dead-gorgeous guy. Big-muscles guy. Supercute guy. Going-to-Princeton-on-an-athletic-scholarship guy.

Her head began to spin. "I don't know where to start!"

Coach Lee squinted at her. "You wouldn't be going into this story with a personal agenda, would you?"

"No, of course not," Riley said quickly. "That would be unprofessional." She glanced down at the image of drop-dead-gorgeous guy. "Let's get started. What's the lowdown on him?"

"That's Brad Collins," Coach Lee said. "He's our star quarterback. A sure bet to go pro one day."

Feeling anxious, Riley glanced at her watch. How could she politely tell Coach Lee that she didn't have time for a whole biography on every player? Basically she just needed to know the name, current dating situation, and whether or not this Saturday was open.

[Riley: I know, you're probably saying, "Where is the romance? Is this girl looking for a date or ordering a sandwich from the deli?" But the clock is ticking! At times like these, a girl can't be choosy. If he's cute and unattached, I'll take him. At this point he doesn't even have to dance that well.]

She suggested to Coach Lee that he just go down the starting lineup with the information she needed. "Otherwise I'll be late for my French class, and Mrs. Lerman always gives a pop quiz during the first five minutes."

Riley shifted uneasily in her chair as Coach Lee ticked off each name and delivered the bad news. Each and every one of these boys seemed to have a girlfriend, and they weren't just regular girls like Riley. They were cheerleaders or so beautiful, they were probably members of the Future Supermodels of America Club or something. A handful of the guys were unattached, but all of them were stuck with community service at the weekend for pulling a prank on a rival school.

Except for one. A huge boy Coach Lee called T-Rex. Named after the dinosaur apparently. He weighed over two hundred and fifty pounds and could block three players at a time during a game. And he liked to roar when doing so.

Riley decided to pass.

chapter
four

"**I**'m dying to read it," Tara was telling Chloe over the phone.

"Yeah, me, too," Amanda Gray said. She was Chloe's very shy friend, and Chloe couldn't believe she had agreed to a three-way call with Tara. Maybe the girl was beginning to come out of her shell.

Chloe giggled. "Everything will be revealed tomorrow morning," she said, enjoying the fact that she had them in suspense. "I will tell you this much – the title of my 'Sound Off' is 'Saturday Sounds Perfect.'"

Chloe was kicked back in her room, switching channels, and fending off Tara and Amanda while waiting for Riley to get home. An anxious feeling settled in the pit of her stomach. The clock was ticking. They needed to get started on finding Mom and Dad dates.

"Come on. Give us a sneak preview!" Tara begged.

"Yeah," Amanda agreed. "Don't make us wait until the school paper comes out. We're your friends."

Just then Riley stepped into the room and announced, "I've got *major* news."

Chloe signed off with the girls and crisscrossed her legs on the bed. "Okay, spill it."

"I found a date for Mom," Riley said proudly.

Chloe could hardly believe it. "Who?"

"Coach Lee," Riley replied.

Chloe *didn't* believe it. "No!"

Riley smiled. "Yes!"

Chloe got off the bed and practically jumped up and down. "This is crazy!" But then she paused to think about it. Coach Lee was about Mom's age, kind of cute, and single. Why not? But there seemed to be one little problem. Chloe's excitement came to a sudden halt. "But don't we have to get them together without letting Mom know that we're getting them together?"

Riley plopped down onto the bed. "I know," she said. That's the hard part." Then she took in an excited breath. "I've got it!"

Chloe's heart picked up speed. "What?"

But just as quickly, Riley's enthusiasm faded. "Never mind. That would never work."

Frustrated, Chloe stood up and began pacing. "Let's put aside Mom for a minute. At least we're halfway there. An idea will come to us. We're just thinking too hard right now. The real problem is Dad! We are *nowhere* on finding him a date."

Riley fell back on the bed as if exhausted. "I walked into this room in a great mood. What happened?"

"Reality set in," Chloe informed her. "Okay, if I were a single woman and met Dad—"

"Yuck. I cannot even think like that," Riley said, scrunching up her face.

Chloe shuddered. "You're right. Too weird." She paced another moment or two. "Let's take a different tack. What are Dad's hobbies? We'll try to find someone with his interests."

"Yeah! Like pen pals or something," Riley said, nodding.

"Exactly," Chloe said. "Okay, we know that he never misses his yoga class."

"And he prides himself on knowing who makes the best granola in Malibu," Riley put in. "Oh! And don't forget his discipline for soulful meditation."

"Or his routine of reading his daily Buddhist wisdom e-mails."

Riley tilted her head. "I forgot about that one." She shut her eyes tight. "Think, Riley, think," she chanted to herself, then let out a heavy sigh before opening her eyes. "I've got nothing."

Chloe had to admit that she was coming up empty, too. She looked down at Pepper, their black-and-white cocker spaniel, who was looking up in expectation of attention. "Pepper, do you have any ideas?"

Pepper's tiny tail wagged back and forth.

Chloe scanned her bedroom, trying to get an idea. Her gaze fell upon the laptop sitting on her desk. Impulsively she booted up and logged on to the Internet. "Maybe we'll find an idea on-line," she said.

"Good thinking," Riley agreed.

Before Chloe could click on to a search engine, one of those annoying pop-up advertisements filled the screen. She huffed. "I get so sick of these..." Her voice trailed off as she realised that the pop-up ad in question was boasting a southern-California-based on-line dating service. Chloe tossed a look to Riley. "I know what we can do for Dad!" she exclaimed.

"What?" Riley asked, rushing to the computer.

"The answer just popped onto the screen!" Chloe exclaimed. "Everybody is finding dates on-line. Why shouldn't Dad?"

By the time the fourth-period bell rang on Wednesday, Chloe's first "Sound Off" column had found its way into the hands of every student at West Malibu High. It was a crazy feeling.

Amanda had already read the article three times. "This is a modern classic for our generation! Whenever my parents argue, my mom makes my dad read *Men Are from Mars, Women Are from Venus* all over again." She paused. "Did I get the planets right?"

Chloe laughed. "I think so."

Amanda glanced upwards, brushing back her

shiny brown hair. "I wonder which planet *boys* are from," she said.

"Probably one of the unidentified ones in another galaxy," Chloe replied.

"Excuse me, aren't you Chloe Carlson?" a girl said.

Chloe spun around to face the voice. It belonged to a pretty junior whom she recognised but had never met. Clutched in the girl's hand was the school newspaper, folded back to reveal the "Sound Off" page. Chloe smiled and nodded.

"I'm Krista, and I just read your article. You go, girl!" she said, pumping her fist in the air.

Another girl moving down the hall in the opposite direction reached out to high-five Chloe. "I couldn't have said it better myself!" she said.

Chloe, stunned by the response, just stood there.

"You have a gift," Amanda said. "Wouldn't it be great if you had your own talk show? You could be the teenage Oprah. Maybe you should look into getting an agent?"

"Uh, no thanks," Chloe said. "This is insane. But it's also kind of a relief. Now I know that it's not just me who thinks boys are lazy when it comes to dating. Obviously other girls feel the same way that I do."

"Exactly," Amanda agreed. "You've definitely struck a chord with the female population." She glanced at a group of boys who were playfully shoving each other and barking like junkyard dogs. "I'm not sure about the other half though. You might have to put it in a rap song to reach them."

"Let's hope not," Chloe said. "I'm no rap artist, that's for sure."

They were just heading into the cafeteria as the first lunch shift was filing out. For a moment it was total body crush. Somewhere in the crowd Chloe spotted Lennon coming towards them. She felt a familiar storm of nervous energy.

Had he read her "Sound Off"? Did he get the picture now? Would he ask her to the Save the Seals benefit?

As the questions piled up in her mind, the mob inched her and Lennon closer and closer together. Finally, just as they reached each other, the crowd opened up. She sighed her relief. At last! Room to breathe.

Amanda announced that she would secure seats at their table and left Chloe to deal with Lennon one-on-one.

Lennon touched Chloe's arm and gently led her to the side, out of the path of comers and goers.

Chloe practically swooned. It was so sweet the way he'd just looked out for her safety and everything.

[Chloe: Don't laugh. I'm serious about this. What Lennon just did was a heroic act. If you've ever been around a bunch of hungry teenagers, you'd know what I'm talking about. Obviously he wants to make certain that I'm safe and sound for the dance on Saturday night!]

As Lennon gazed at her and gave her that cute, lopsided grin of his, Chloe tossed her soft, wavy curls. She had planned for it to be a smooth, movie star type of move. Unfortunately several strands landed in her face and stuck to her lip gloss. She quickly swiped them back.

"A word of caution," Lennon said. "Despite the bad press, the pizza has shown no signs of improvement."

Chloe laughed a little. "Thanks for the warning." Her mind raced. Lennon had just made a direct reference to the "Sound Off" column. Not hers, of course, but maybe this was his way of letting her know that he had read it. Chloe glanced away and then back again, waiting for him to say something else.

"Well," he finally murmured. "I'd better get to class." He started to go.

Chloe stood there, stunned. "That's all you have to say?" This question had been meant for just inside her confused head, but somehow it had come sputtering out of her mouth.

Lennon appeared genuinely puzzled. "Oh… um…you look cute today."

Chloe couldn't help but smile her thanks. That was a start, but she had been expecting much more. Finally she decided to simply come out with it. "Did you happen to read my column in the newspaper today?"

"Oh, yeah," Lennon said, his face brightening.

"Congratulations on that. It must be cool to see your name in print. I'll see you later." And that was it. He was gone.

Chloe stood there, replaying the scene all over again in her mind. No, this wasn't a nightmare. It had actually happened that way.

Amanda came rushing up to her. "Your column is a runaway hit! *Everybody* is talking about it."

"Whoop-dee-do," Chloe mumbled. "Right now I'd settle for just one person in particular getting the point of it."

chapter
five

Riley and Sierra Pomeroy were in the cafeteria reading Chloe's "Sound Off" column together, stopping to recite their favourite parts out loud. After which, they'd break up into fits of laughter.

Sierra's double life never ceased to amaze Riley. Her real name was Sarah, given to her by strict and old-fashioned parents. They would freak if they ever knew that she went by Sierra, changed into wild clothes before first period, and played bass guitar in The Wave, the same band that Riley's old boyfriend, Alex, was a member of. Small world. Especially since Sierra was dating Larry Slotnick, Riley's neighbour.

> [Riley: I have to confess. Watching Larry get over me and enter the dating world hasn't been the easiest thing to deal with. I mean, Larry's had a crush on me since the first grade. As far as stalkers go, he wasn't so bad.

I used to wish he would leave me alone, but at times like these I actually miss the way he used to ask me out every five minutes. At least somebody was interested in me!]

"Lennon has to ask Chloe to Save the Seals now," Sierra said. "Because if he doesn't, I would *not* want to be the one who lives with Chloe Carlson this week."

"He will," Riley said. She was sure of it in fact. But what she wasn't sure of was her own date. "Okay, Chloe is covered, we've got a plan for Mom, the situation for Dad is in the works, and here I am, stuck." Her light mood turned sullen on a dime. "Watch me be the only one without a date."

"Think positive," Sierra said. "Let's work this out like a maths problem." She reached into her messenger bag, pulled out a pad of graph paper, and began scratching out what looked to be a flowchart.

Riley was totally confused. "Exactly what are you doing?" she asked.

"Making sure that you cover all the bases," Sierra said, continuing to mark up the paper. "Let's factor out all possible guy types. For instance, we have the jocks." She scribbled the word on the paper.

Riley shook her head. "Draw a line through that one. There are no possibilities. Except T-Rex. And I won't consider that option until Sunday morning."

Sierra glanced up. "But the dance is Saturday night."

"My point exactly," Riley said.

Sierra laughed. "What about the cool kids?"

"Most of them are holding tickets to the Tribal Council concert. Besides, Save the Seals is not exactly known for its wild mosh pit. And parents will be there, too. The cool crowd would have big problems with that."

Sierra scratched through category number two. "All's not lost. We've got the brainiacs."

"Not this weekend," Riley said. "They leave Friday for the Olympics of the Mind regional finals in San Francisco. Won't be back until Monday."

Sierra inspected her nails. "Okay, I wouldn't normally suggest this, but every girl gets a crush on at least one, so why not get it out of your system?"

Riley leaned in towards the table, intrigued now. "What are you talking about?"

Sierra grinned. "Bad boys."

Riley laughed. "I can't go out with a bad boy! It would never work. You're looking at a girl who feels like a criminal when she doesn't rewind movies before returning them to Blockbuster."

"You have a point." Sierra sighed, eliminating category number four. "We're down to fashion extremists."

"That includes the Goths, right?"

Sierra nodded. "And guys with multiple piercings."

"I'll pass. Not interested in boys who wear more makeup than I do." Riley paused a beat. "Or more jewellery."

Sierra groaned and glanced helplessly at her chart. "Riles, you've got to work with me here. The only category left is, well, *Larry*."

Riley giggled. "Yeah. Larry definitely belongs in his own category."

"But he's taking me to the movies on Saturday," Sierra pointed out. "As *friends*."

Riley gave Sierra a strange look. "Why did you say it like that?"

"Because we broke up last week," Sierra said.

Riley's mouth dropped open in shock. "What? When were you going to tell me?"

Sierra shrugged. "I just did."

"Why did you guys break up?" Riley asked. "I thought you liked each other."

"Don't get me wrong," Sierra said. "Larry's a great guy, but he's just not for me. Besides, all he does is talk about *you*."

"Oh," Riley muttered, feeling a little guilty. But then this got her thinking. She and Alex had broken up recently as well. Maybe they could go as friends, too. Why not? "I'll ask Alex," she announced all of a sudden. "He's still trying to pay off his new guitar, so I'm sure he didn't splurge on Tribal Council tickets. I'll bet he's free. He'd probably love to go to a big dance party."

Sierra directed her gaze behind Riley. "Well, here he comes. Why don't you ask him?"

Riley twisted around to see Alex's lanky, future rock star frame walk towards them – and past them –

without a word, although he did acknowledge Sierra with a friendly nod.

"Did you see what just happened?" Riley shrieked. "Alex completely ignored me. That could easily go down as the insult heard throughout the lunchroom."

"Don't take it personally," Sierra said. "It's not Alex's fault."

Riley narrowed her eyes. Alex's behaviour was confusing enough. But Sierra saying it wasn't his fault made no sense at all. "Excuse me?"

"It's called cool-guy-disorder. Happens after every breakup. They suddenly have to act like they're so *over it*. You know, basically pretend like you don't exist. In a few weeks it will all be over."

Riley rolled her eyes. "Oh, I can't wait." She paused. "Did L*arry* do this to you?"

Sierra shook her head. "He doesn't have the gene. Not cool enough."

"Lucky you."

Without warning Sierra slapped the table with a jewelled hand.

Everybody jolted.

"Do *you* have a disorder we should know about?" Riley asked.

"Yes, it's called *brilliance*," Sierra said. "I can't believe I forgot this category! It's the perfect one for you."

Riley couldn't stand the suspense. "Tell me! What?"

"Exchange students," Sierra said grandly. "What do you think about Jacques, that dreamy guy from France?"

"Hello?" Riley shouted. "He's only like a walking beautification project for West Malibu High." She scanned the lunchroom. "Where is he?"

Sierra laughed. "Calm down, Mademoiselle. He doesn't eat lunch during this period."

"I'll ask him," Riley decided. "I mean, it's important to reach out to our international friends. You know, make them feel at home."

After school at California Dream, Riley sipped on a Vanilla Coke and tried to cheer up Chloe, who was looking pretty depressed slumped in the opposite chair. She had told the story of Lennon not asking her to the dance at least three times already.

"I think we're the only girls at West Malibu who don't have dates for Saturday night," Chloe was saying. "Tara's going out with that cute guy who left West Malibu to be home schooled, and Amanda's got a date with a trombone player from the Santa Monica High marching band."

Riley slurped her soda all the way to the bottom of the glass. "I told you about Sierra and Larry, right?"

Chloe nodded.

"Well, I was thinking about asking Jacques, the guy from France," Riley said.

Chloe shook her head sullenly. "Too late. Quinn

asked him out during study hall, and he said yes."

"Ugh!" Riley gave up and put her head down on the table. She glanced around the place, half expecting a magic answer to materialise out of thin air. And one practically did.

Across the room she noticed a new poster plastered on the wall. The super-cute surfer boy on it caught her eye. She erupted from her chair and dashed over to get a closer look.

The boy was named C.J. Logan and the poster was for the first annual Waverider International surfing competition. Of course! Riley had known it was coming up soon. Suddenly her heart bolted in her chest. She had a great idea!

Glancing back at the table, Riley made a wild gesture for Chloe to come over in a hurry. When her sister joined her, Riley pointed at the poster as if it explained everything.

Chloe seemed unimpressed. "That is not a cute boy. That is a *poster* of a cute boy."

"Don't you get it?" Riley demanded. "The competition is going on right now. C.J. Logan is actually in Malibu as we speak."

Chloe's expression was blank. "Who is C.J. Logan?"

Riley's focus bounced back to the poster. "He's from Australia. He's fifteen years old. And he's a total hottie. I can't believe I was upset about Quinn asking out Jacques."

"You shouldn't be," Chloe said. "French boys are so five minutes ago. Besides, I have it on good authority that he needs to be introduced to a wonderful invention called the TicTac."

Riley giggled, then turned her attention back to the Waverider poster. C.J. Logan was amazing. A surfing whiz *and* an Aussie accent! Now all she had to do was figure out a plan to meet him *and* ask him to go to Save the Seals.

chapter
six

"This is exactly why they invented the phrase, Could things get any *more* complicated?" Chloe whispered to her sister.

It was Wednesday afternoon. Their mom was busy fitting her friend and supermodel, Tedi, for a new dress. Manuelo was front and centre in the kitchen, explaining his own dating issues.

"So you see," Manuelo continued, "I couldn't help it. I'm such a good cook that my meals-in-a-minute went for big money at the Dinner at Eight auction. All the proceeds go to the local theatre, which is good. But now the chairperson of the fund-raiser believes an invitation to Save the Seals is a great way to thank me, which is bad. Why? Because I don't have a date."

"Neither do I," Chloe said.

"Ditto," Riley added.

Manuelo ignored them. "Look at this," he whined, holding up the glossy invitation. "It says 'Manuelo Del

Valle plus one.'" He frowned. "I have no plus one. It's just me. Manuelo. All alone. So sad. So very, very sad." He looked at Chloe and Riley with pleading puppy-dog eyes.

Chloe sighed. "Don't cry, Manuelo. We'll find you a date. We promise."

Manuelo's mood went into fast turnaround. "Really? This is wonderful, girls. Thank you, thank you, thank you. I'd better get this reply card in the mail right away." He started humming a song and disappeared through the kitchen doorway.

Riley tugged on Chloe's sleeve. "You do realise that we have to find five dates by Saturday. And keep in mind that between the two of us, we can't even seem to find one."

"But what was I supposed to say?" Chloe asked. "He looked liked he was about to cry. Besides, if all of us went to the dance and Manuelo stayed home, it wouldn't be as much fun."

Riley nodded. "I guess you're right. But you have to admit, this is getting ridiculous."

"That's the understatement of the week," Chloe said.

"So what are we going to do about Manuelo?" Riley asked.

Chloe stepped over to the freezer, opened the door, and just let the chill wash over her. Finding Dad a date, finding Manuelo a date, and, how could she forget, finding *herself* a date. Not to mention something cute to wear. This would be one tough order to fill.

"Is the answer behind the Ben and Jerry's?" Riley teased.

"If only it were that simple." Chloe said. She grabbed a pint of Chunky Monkey and shut the door. Maybe all the calories would generate some inspiration.

That same day in the early evening Riley discovered Tedi standing on a small stool in the living room. She was wearing a form-fitting animal print number that featured a daring slit up the side. "Wow, Tedi! You look amazing!" she said.

Tedi smiled. "Thank you. It's too conservative for Jennifer Lopez, but for a simple girl like me, it's truly wild." She glanced around and zeroed in on the clock. "Your mother left me stranded to take a phone call, and I have an eyebrow waxing in forty-five minutes." She sighed. "But she's making me look fabulous for the Model of the Year Awards, so I won't complain too much."

"Can I get you anything while you're waiting?" Riley asked.

"Would you please hand me that *People* over there on the coffee table?" Tedi asked. "Since I'm stuck here, I should probably read something educational."

Riley passed her the magazine.

Tedi studied the cover. "Oh, good. The best-and-worst-dressed list."

Riley smiled to herself and settled in on the sofa, tucking her feet underneath her legs. Suddenly it occurred to her that Tedi might have some valuable insight on how to reel in a super-hottie like C.J. Logan. "Hey, did Mom mention that we were taking dates to Save the Seals this year?"

Tedi closed the magazine and gave Riley a bright smile. "Yes, she did! So tell me. Who's the lucky guy?"

"That's the trouble. I don't know yet."

Tedi's face registered a moment's pure horror. "You don't know? Isn't the dance this weekend?"

Riley nodded.

"Sweetie, by this point in the week you should be trying to decide on lip colour, not who's going to take you!"

"But the boy I want to go with doesn't even know I'm alive."

"If this guy hasn't taken notice of a beautiful girl like you, then he's not worth the trouble."

"No, you don't understand," Riley said. "He *really* doesn't know that I'm alive. We've never met."

"Oh," Tedi said. She thought for a moment then shrugged. "Well, introduce yourself. I'm sure he'll fall madly in love."

Riley shifted in her seat. "It's a little more complicated than that. He's sort of…well, he's sort of famous."

Tedi widened her eyes. "Famous? Sweetie, you're not talking about Prince William, are you?"

Riley shook her head.

"Prince Harry?" Tedi wondered.

Riley laughed. "Nobody in the royal family, Tedi. He's a surfer, one of the youngest competitors ever, and he's taking part in the Waverider International."

"Isn't that going on right now?" Tedi asked.

"Yes," Riley answered. "But how do I get his attention? I mean, this event is huge, and there are probably hundreds of girls who want to meet him."

Tedi glanced around, then stepped off the stool in a huff. "At the very least I hope your mother's on the phone with the President or First Lady." She smoothed out her dress and gingerly settled on the sofa next to Riley. "You came to the right girl for this. Famous men are my specialty. Did I ever tell you the story about Sam Law, the lead singer for Blowtorch?"

Riley shook her head no. She knew the band though. Blowtorch was a regular fixture on MTV, and Sam Law's name always turned up in the celebrity gossip mill. Women fell over themselves just to get close to him.

"Like every other woman in this hemisphere, I had a mad crush on the man. But unlike them, I wasn't going to try my chances at meeting him backstage. Famous guy rule number one: Meet professionally on his turf. I went after a part in the new Blowtorch video and got it, so we were introduced on the set by the director."

"What happened next?" Riley demanded.

"It was a two-day shoot. Our first date was at the wrap party. For the next three weeks we were madly in love – which is pretty much a silver anniversary for rock stars and models – and then it was over." Tedi stared into space for a few seconds. "I can't remember what happened exactly. I just know that we got into a huge argument, and I ended up throwing a banana daiquiri into his lap. Haven't heard from him since. Oh, well." She patted Riley's knee. "So tell me about this guy."

Riley smiled brightly as thoughts of C.J. Logan took flight in her mind. "Well, he's a surfer from Australia—"

"Which is good," Tedi cut in. "That means we know in advance that he's cute with a great tan, perfect body and a killer accent."

"That's for sure," Riley said.

Tedi tapped a manicured nail to her painted lips. "Can you surf?"

"Sort of. But not well enough to compete."

"Okay," Tedi went on, concentrating hard. "What can you do that would get you to that competition in an official way?"

The perfect solution flashed in Riley's mind. "I can interview him for the sports section of the school paper!"

Tedi clapped her hands. "Sweetie, *you* are thinking like *me*." She paused. "How old are you?"

"Fourteen," Riley replied.

"That's what I thought. Promise me you won't think like me again for several years. Better to quit while you're ahead."

Riley laughed and shot up from the sofa, eager to fill Chloe in on her new plan. "I promise." She started out, then halted, wondering if Tedi might be a strong ally to encourage Mom to go out with Coach Lee. "Tedi, has Mom mentioned anything to you about finding a date for Save the Seals?"

A frustrated breath escaped Tedi. "Don't get me started on your mother. I've offered to set her up with a great guy, but she refuses to let anyone help her find a date. Honestly, I've given up."

"Given up on what?" Macy asked as she bounded back into the room.

Tedi rose from the sofa and took her position on the stool once again. "Finding you a date for Save the Seals."

Macy waved off the subject. "I'm sorry my call took so long. The buyer in Milan just wanted to talk and talk." She surveyed the dress with pinpoint accuracy. "I should take it in about an eighth of an inch at the waist. Other than that, it fits like a glove."

"And feels like a corset," Tedi said. "Remind me not to breathe in this dress. But back to this dating business…"

"No," Macy said, holding up a hand. "I can find my own date, thank you very much."

"By the way, how's that working out?" Tedi asked.

Macy's cheeks blushed a faint pink. "Not so well."

Riley saw an opening and decided to go for it. "You know, Mom, there's a teacher at West Malibu who would love to go to the dance. His name is—"

"I'm not interested, Riley. Besides, aren't you and your sister supposed to find a date for your father?" Macy asked.

"Yes," Riley answered.

"Then concentrate on that," she replied. "I'll figure out something on my own."

"So will I," Riley murmured under her breath. And then she left the living room in search of Chloe. There had to be a way to trick Mom into meeting Coach Lee!

chapter
seven

[Chloe: Last evening I went to bed with finding a date for Manuelo on my mind. In the middle of the night I dreamed about Lennon asking me out. This morning I woke up to see a Post-it note on my laptop that read, Update dad's on-line dating profile. Okay, is it just me, or has all this dating business completely taken over our lives? Oh, by the way, in my dream Lennon asked me out all by himself. No hints. No clues planted in newspaper columns. Just a boy with a little bit of romantic nerve. It was an awesome dream.]

Chloe booted up her laptop and went straight to work on her dad's on-line dating profile. She studied the original version with a critical eye and decided that ultimately listing all of his earth-guy qualities just wasn't enough to get women interested.

Granted, her dad was a truly impressive guy but on paper he didn't seem that way. One could even argue that he was just an unemployed trailer park resident. Not exactly bachelor-of-the-year material.

Chloe punched up the answers a bit. After all, a little creativity never hurt. Now Dad was an "entrepreneur in between projects who enjoys coastal living." She smiled at her handiwork and e-mailed the application to the dating service.

All she had to do was wait for Dad's special cyber mailbox to fill up. Hopefully it would. In a hurry!

"Mom," Riley said, staring into her bowl of cereal, "would you mind dropping me off at school and coming into the office for a minute? The secretary needs you to sign a form so I can leave campus to cover the Waverider competition for the newspaper." She didn't dare lift her head now. Her left eye was twitching like crazy, and her mom would know for certain that she was lying.

Luckily her mom was too busy punching buttons on her Palm Pilot to take notice.

"No problem," Macy replied. "But we should probably leave in a few minutes. I'm due at a trunk show in Santa Monica and I don't want to be late."

Riley deposited her bowl in the sink and dashed upstairs to gather her things for school. She stopped in on Chloe, who was still hard at work on the Internet. "How's it going?"

Chloe beamed triumphant. "I just posted Dad's new profile a few minutes ago and there are already three responses. Imagine how many there will be when we get home from school! What about you?"

Riley brought her voice down to a faint whisper. "Mom doesn't suspect a thing yet," she told her sister. "Wish me luck."

Chloe crossed her fingers on both hands.

"Riley!" Mom called from downstairs. "Are you almost ready?"

"Coming!" Riley waved good-bye to Chloe and dashed to the car. The short ride to school was easy. A fashion reporter had called Mom on her mobile phone for an interview about Tedi's Model of the Year Awards dress. While Mom wrapped up the conversation, Riley rushed into the school office to put the finishing touches on her scheme, praying that it would work.

"Good morning, Riley! It's going to be another great day at West Malibu High!" Rebecca Ravitz said as soon as she saw Riley.

The too-eager voice rattled Riley for a moment. Rebecca was the biggest gossip in the ninth-grade class, and, as luck would have it, she was the morning office assistant, too.

"Hi, Rebecca," Riley said, keeping her voice low so that none of the teachers or administrators milling about would hear. "I was hoping you could help me with something."

"Help you with something?" Rebecca asked curiously. "No problem. What is it?"

"Could you please page Coach Lee to the office." Riley's gaze darted to the door. There was still no sign of Mom. Good.

"Why do you need me to page Coach Lee?" Rebecca asked. She narrowed her eyes.

Riley glanced nervously at the adults in the room, then relaxed. Nobody seemed to be paying attention. "I can't explain right now, Rebecca, but it's very, very important."

Rebecca grabbed the intercom system and pressed a red button. "Coach Lee to the office, Coach Lee to the office! This is an emergency! Lives are at stake! Every second that goes by is the tick tock of danger! Coach Lee to the office!" And then she smiled. "There. That should get him here."

Riley buried her face in her hands. What was Rebecca *doing*?

Mom rushed into the office. "Is everything okay?"

Then Coach Lee burst onto the scene, running smack dab into Mom. "Excuse me, ma'am, I'm terribly sorry," he apologised, steadying her shoulders with both hands. And then he did a double take, smiling all of a sudden.

"Oh, I'm fine. Really, I am," Mom said, clearing her throat as she nervously finger-combed her hair.

Coach Lee extended his hand. "I should probably introduce myself since I almost knocked you down. I'm

George Lee. I coach football and teach health here at West Malibu."

Macy shook his hand firmly, and Riley noticed that her hold of it lingered for a moment. "Macy Carlson. I'm—"

"Chloe and Riley's mother," the coach said. "Of course you are. I can see the resemblance. You have lovely girls."

Macy smiled. "Why, thank you…*George*."

"Call me Coach."

"Very well…*Coach*."

Riley watched all of this from just a few feet away. She had counted on some sparks, but this was an electrical storm. A total love connection! Getting Mom a date was going to be easier than she thought!

Riley's celebration came to a crashing halt as soon as Ms. Raffin entered the office.

"Good morning, Mrs. Carlson. How nice to see you. What brings you here this morning?" Ms. Raffin said.

Riley spun around to avoid eye contact and once more came face-to-face with Rebecca.

"This is getting interesting," Rebecca said. "Do you need me to page someone else?"

Yes, Riley wanted to say, a helicopter to get me out of here! But she remained silent instead, listening in on every word of the conversations behind her.

"Riley is so excited about covering the surfing competition for the school paper," Mom was saying. "I just came in to sign the permission forms for her to leave school early."

"I have no idea what you're talking about," Ms. Raffin said.

"Rebecca, who had me paged?" Coach Lee asked.

"Riley," Rebecca said, pointing at her.

Riley could feel the heat of Mom's gaze burning into her back, and she knew that Ms. Raffin and Coach Lee were staring as well. One thing was certain – she would definitely have some explaining to do.

> [Riley: You probably think I'm in serious trouble, don't you? Well, okay, I am. Things aren't as bad as they seem. Really. The way I figure it, no harm, no foul. Nobody was hurt and nothing was broken. Everybody will probably have a good laugh about this at some point in the future. Hopefully that will be a few minutes from now.]

"Riley, Ms. Raffin and I would appreciate some clarification on a few matters," Mom said.

Bracing herself for the worst, Riley turned around to face them, laughing nervously. "You know, it's the funniest thing. I may have forgotten to talk to Ms. Raffin about this assignment."

"'*May* have'?" Ms. Raffin echoed. "I would definitely remember such a conversation."

Coach Lee had a puzzled expression on his face. "Will someone please tell me why I was paged to the office?"

"To meet me, I'm afraid," Mom said, figuring out the whole thing. "I think my daughter had a little plan up her sleeve this morning."

Coach Lee flashed a charming smile. "Is that so? Well, I'd like to go on record as saying that I admire your daughter's plan. It introduced me to you."

Mom was genuinely taken aback. "I suppose it was harmless enough."

Ms. Raffin stepped toward Riley. "What's this about a surfing competition?"

Riley quickly explained what the Waverider was, the significance of C.J. Logan being the youngest participant, and how great it would be to do a piece on him for the paper.

Ms. Raffin smiled wide. "This is exactly what I love to see in my reporters – a knack for ideas that are outside the box. Bring back the story. Photos, too."

Riley nodded dutifully, hardly able to contain her excitement.

"Oh, and, Riley," Ms. Raffin added, "please remember that this is for the *sports* page. Your last article about the football team turned out to be more of a dating survey than an athletic feature."

"Yes, Ms. Raffin," Riley said. Then she glanced over to observe Mom and Coach Lee. They were exchanging phone numbers and, from the sound of it, planning a mixed doubles tennis date for later in the afternoon. This last development left Riley completely stunned. Mom didn't know the

so little time

first thing about tennis!

I guess Mom must really like Coach Lee. Riley grinned to herself. Cool.

chapter eight

Chloe ducked into the Newsstand with hopes of running into Lennon before school. Unfortunately there was no sign of him. Disappointed, she waited in line for a hot chocolate.

The girl behind the counter was brand new and very slow. Finally Chloe got her steamy cocoa and started out. Just as she approached the door, she did a double take. Lennon *was* at the Newsstand. He was sitting alone at a corner table, hunched over a book and facing the wall.

Chloe crept up behind him. "Do you want some company, or are you being antisocial?" she asked.

Lennon twisted around and broke into a smile. "Hey, how are you?"

She slipped into the chair opposite him and sighed heavily. "Do you really want to know?"

"That bad?" He gestured to the book he was reading. "Is it worse than trying to learn everything about the Trojan War in twenty minutes?"

Chloe wondered if that was a hint for her to scram so he could study. She hesitated. "Maybe I should—"

"No, stick around." Lennon closed the book and stuffed it into his backpack. "What's up?"

"I'll be so glad when this weekend is over with," Chloe admitted, "and if it doesn't come soon, then Save the Seals just might become Save Chloe."

Lennon cracked a smile. "That's the big dance on Saturday, right?"

"Yes," Chloe said. This was close. She could feel it. He *had* to ask her now! "My parents are separated and refuse to go together, so Riley and I are trying to find dates for them, trying to find dates for ourselves, and, as of last night, trying to find a date for our housekeeper." She let out a heavy sigh. "But so far nobody has a date. And it's Thursday."

Lennon chuckled. "That's pretty funny."

Chloe sat there in expectant silence, waiting for more.

But nothing came. Lennon might as well have been a statue in the park. He made no sound and showed no signs of life.

Finally he gathered up his things to leave. "I guess we'd better start heading out."

"You go ahead without me," Chloe said in a snappy tone. "There's something I've got to do first." Every time she brought up the dance, Lennon either ignored the subject or changed it altogether! Maybe a quick mood swing would get his attention.

But just like he was with everything else that Chloe seemed to say or do, Lennon remained unfazed. "Okay," he murmured with a shrug and took off.

Chloe took a long drink of her cocoa as if she'd find the secret of life at the bottom of the cup. Actually she'd settle for something much more simple. Like the answer to the single question going through her mind: what was Lennon's problem?

Ugh! This playing-dumb act of his was really getting old. They'd already been out on a date, and she *thought* that he liked her. But if he didn't, why couldn't he just make it official – in person, on the phone, by e-mail? I just want to be friends. That's *all* he had to say.

Chloe sat there, her emotions totally mixed up. One second she was riddled with insecurity, and the next second she was filled with fury. All the back-and-forth had her head spinning!

Why don't boys ever just say what they feel! she wanted to scream. Whoa. She needed to chill. No boy was worth this much drama.

No matter, Chloe couldn't help wondering. Why was Lennon doing this? Did he enjoy watching her make a fool of herself? Or was he really that clueless? Well, Chloe didn't care any more. As of that moment, her days of playing Little Miss Please-Ask-Me-to-the-Dance were officially over. That's right!

From then on boys were going to fall over

themselves to ask her out on dates. Otherwise she just wouldn't bother. The thought amused her. Wouldn't that be great? A world where every boy you liked instantly asked you out for Saturday night? Or if a guy *wasn't* interested, he *told* you straight up – instead of pretending he liked you for whatever reason.

Really. Guys were so immature sometimes.

Chloe smiled, thinking of all the girls at school who appreciated her first "Sound Off." They would definitely love this scenario.

Inspired, she left the table, settled in at one of the empty cyber stations, and began composing another "Sound Off." She called this one "Saturday Sounds Perfect Part II." After all, the first one was a hit, and everybody loved a sequel.

The column practically wrote itself. Her fingers flitted across the keyboard at a breakneck pace. Within minutes she was done. On a lark she e-mailed the piece to Ms. Raffin with a brief note. Maybe there would be space for a last-minute article in Friday's edition of the paper.

Chloe was logging off the system, when she noticed a stray flyer screaming the banner headline: IF YOU DON'T BELIEVE IN LOVE AT FIRST SIGHT, HOW ABOUT LOVE IN FIVE MINUTES?

She picked it up to discover that the Newsstand was hosting a speed-dating session – that night. She had seen a story about it once on a morning show. It sounded kind of cool. Instead of a single blind date that lasts a few hours, you sign up for speed dating, a series of eight mini blind dates that would last five to ten minutes.

Chloe folded the flyer and slipped it into the front pocket of her backpack. That just might be the perfect plan for Manuelo!

The Waverider thrummed with action and Riley was totally excited to be in the midst of it. Surfers from all over the world were there, not to mention top corporate sponsors, trainers, media pros and hordes of fans.

Riley fingered the credentials hanging around her neck. Her laminated pass read PRESS – ALL ACCESS, and it was attached to a thick black cord. She looked *very* official. Ms. Raffin had made last minute arrangements. As it happened, one of her former students was managing the press tent.

Today's waves were no joke. In fact Riley had never seen them so huge. She watched in awe as each group of surfers skated across the water, instinctively riding the edge of the wave, staying just ahead of the foamy crest. They were like superheroes. It was totally amazing to see.

The wind whipped, the sun beat down, and the tang of the salt water burned in Riley's throat. She had been lucky enough to see C.J. Logan in all three of his heats. Unfortunately he lost to two Americans and another Australian. But for a fifteen-year-old in his first professional competition, he proved himself a force to be reckoned with. The announcers even praised him as a "red-hot kid on the rise" and a "young surfer to watch in the years ahead."

After much hand wringing and nervous pacing, Riley found the nerve to introduce herself to C.J. and request an interview. Now seemed to be the perfect time. All of his heats were over, and he was just hanging out on the beach, scoping out what remained of the competitive action.

"Excuse me," Riley said. But her voice had barely registered above a whisper.

C.J. didn't hear. His gaze remained glued to the two daredevils braving the brutal Pacific waves.

Riley cleared her throat and C.J. glanced over.

"Excuse me," Riley said, much louder this time. "I'm a reporter for West Malibu High. I'd love to interview you for our school paper."

C.J. stepped over in his body-hugging wet suit. "What's your name, mate?"

Riley swallowed hard. The boy was even cuter in person and she loved the Aussie accent! "Riley Carlson," she managed to say, extending her hand.

"C.J. Logan," he said.

His hand was wet and sandy, but Riley didn't care. "You were amazing out there."

C.J. gave a modest shrug. "Wasn't my best day."

Riley fired off a battery of basic profile questions – where C.J. had been born, how long he'd been surfing, and what his goals for the future were. His answers were snappy and funny. At the end she pulled out her digital camera and asked permission to take a picture.

C.J. winked at her. "Only if you're in the picture, too."

Before Riley had a chance to answer, C.J. had called over Joey B., another popular surfer from Australia, to snap the photo. Riley gave Joey B. a quick lesson on how to operate the camera. Then she took her place beside C.J., who draped his arm around her for the shot.

Riley was swooning big time. She didn't want the afternoon to end. C.J. was superfunny, supernice, and supercool! The chemistry between them was natural, as if they'd known each other for a long time.

"I'll be staying in Malibu through Sunday," C.J. said. "Any chance I might see you again?"

Riley's mind raced ahead to Saturday night. She imagined C.J. all dressed up and showing off his moves on the dance floor. "I think that can be arranged."

"How about a surf date tomorrow?" C.J. asked.

Riley stared into the brilliant blue of his eyes. "What's that?"

"I'll show you some long boarding moves, we'll eat a snack on the beach, and then we'll watch the sunset."

Riley hesitated. It sounded like a dream! But part

of her thought about Vance and wondered if it was the right thing to do. Whenever she saw him in the halls, she got a funny feeling in her stomach, and she secretly wished that his cousin had never come up with those tickets to the Tribal Council concert.

In the end, though, she reasoned that they weren't exactly a couple yet. Besides, he was busy with his plans. Why should she sit around like crabgrass? A girl was entitled to her own fun, right?

C.J. tilted his head. "Do we have a date?"

"Yes," Riley said. "In fact, I can't think of anything I'd rather do more."

chapter
nine

Chloe had opened the fridge to get a snack, when her mother walked...well, *stumbled* into the kitchen.

"I don't know what's hurting me more, the blisters on my hands, the blisters on my feet, or every joint and muscle in my body."

Chloe's dad was sitting at the kitchen table. He took a monster bite out of an apple and laughed at Macy. "Sounds like it was a torture session, not a date," he said.

Macy bristled at the joke. "No. It was a *date*," she insisted. "Coach maintains a very active lifestyle. That's a healthy way to live."

Jake shook his head, grinning. He gestured to Chloe's laptop on the counter. "No thanks. I'd rather relax and let women find me on the Internet." He turned to Chloe. "By the way, how's my favourite dating detective coming along with our project?"

Chloe grabbed a yogurt and shut the refrigerator.

"I'm happy to report that your cyber mailbox is full of messages from interested women."

Jake threw a puzzled look over to Macy. "I have no idea what that means, but it sounds good, doesn't it?"

Mom struggled to the table and sat down with a sigh of relief. "Just be careful, Jake. I've heard some pretty crazy on-line dating stories."

"If I didn't know any better, I'd say you were jealous," Jake said, folding his arms.

"Trust me," Macy said, "you don't know any better. Anyway, why would I be jealous? I've got my own date. In fact, Coach is taking me rock climbing tomorrow."

"Rock climbing?" Jake exclaimed. "Macy, you're so scared of heights that you won't even change a lightbulb!"

"I'm not that bad," she protested.

Chloe stared at her mom. Dad was right. Mom was a total chicken when it came to heights.

Macy shrugged. "Well, even if I am that bad, Coach says it's important to face fears of physical challenges."

"Is that so?" Jake said with a smile. "Well, I'll be at the trailer practicing the tango in case anybody needs me." He turned to Chloe. "How does tomorrow night sound for final selection?"

Chloe nodded. "Perfect." She led him over to the laptop. "Look at all these messages in your on-line mailbox. First we have to go through these and decide which ones you want to meet."

Dad was peering over her shoulder, squinting at the screen. "All those are for me?"

"Yes," Chloe said. She clicked the update button. Two more messages popped into the box. "Now there are eighty-six."

"Eighty-six? That's a lot of mail to read. I'm still trying to get through last week's *Buddhist Today* magazine."

Chloe peered up at her father. "Well, I guess Riley and I could weed out the undesirables and set up a meet and greet with the top contenders."

"That sounds great, honey," Jake said. "Well, I'd better run."

As Jake left, Manuelo rushed into the kitchen carrying three sacks of groceries.

"Hello, hello, hello," he sang breathlessly. "Traffic is a nightmare. I should have started dinner over an hour ago. I hope nobody's hungry. We're having paella tonight. An old family recipe. Trust me. It'll be worth the wait. So stop complaining! That means everybody." He bent over to address Pepper. "Including you." Manuelo stood up and noticed Mom's disheveled state. "What happened to you?"

"I had a tennis date."

"Why?" Manuelo asked. "Tennis isn't your game. Can you even play Ping-Pong?"

Macy eased herself onto her feet. "Very funny."

"Thank you," Manuelo said. "I'll be here all week."

"I'm going to soak in a nice hot bath before

dinner," Macy said, and shuffled out of the room.

Manuelo began unpacking the groceries. "Where's Riley?"

"She's covering the Waverider for the school paper."

"Ah, the Waverider," Manuelo murmured. "That's part of the reason why I sat in traffic so long. There are cars up and down the beach for miles."

"Oh, I almost forgot," Chloe said. "I've got something for you." She dug deep into her backpack until she found the flyer.

"I hope it's a deed to a French chalet," Manuelo joked.

"It's something better." Chloe unfolded the paper and presented it to him with a flourish. "Ta-da! Your secret dating weapon."

Manuelo scanned the page and frowned. "Speed dating? I don't think so."

Chloe grabbed a spoon from a drawer and opened her yogurt. "Why not? I think it's a great idea."

"Blind dates are risky enough. And you expect me to go on eight of them? No way. I'll take my chances with just one," Manuelo said.

"But what if it's bad?" Chloe said. "It could last for hours. The great thing about speed dating is that the bad ones are over in a matter of minutes."

Manuelo seemed to think this over. "That *is* a better way of looking at it."

"Don't worry. It'll turn out fine," Chloe assured him.

"In fact, Riley and I will go along for moral support. Okay?"

"You promise?" Manuelo asked.

"I promise," Chloe said. After all, the odds were against her having a date for the dance. At least she could get one for Manuelo, right?

The next morning Chloe passed through the doors of West Malibu High and received a round of instant applause.

"You must be reading my mind," one girl said.

"Guys are so clueless!" another girl cried.

A trio of truly appreciative sophomores began chanting, "Go, Chloe, go Chloe, go Chloe!"

"What's up?" she wondered aloud to herself as much as to anyone.

Tara and Quinn came rushing up to her, waving Friday's edition of the school paper. "Oops…you did it again," they sang.

Chloe grabbed it and immediately turned to the "Sound Off" section. She couldn't believe it. "Saturday Sounds Perfect Part II" took up most of the page. Seeing her own work in print and knowing that so many of the girls liked it made her feel great.

"Hey, Chloe," one girl said. "My boyfriend never takes me to the movies. All he wants to do is sit at my house and play Nintendo. What should I do?"

Chloe thought fast for the perfect answer.

so little time

"Practise his favourite game. Once you beat him, he'll never want to play again."

Everybody laughed.

Chloe enjoyed being the witty girl with all the right answers. For a moment, at least, it helped her forget about how upset she was with Lennon. "Girls, always remember this: Who needs boys when you've got a supportive sisterhood?" She tried to sound upbeat, but a hint of sadness crept in.

Tara seemed to pick up on it. "Hey, she's right. If a guy is not digging you, it's *his* loss."

chapter
ten

"**N**ot too shabby, wouldn't you say, mate?" C.J. said, proudly displaying the complimentary Waverider surfboard that he received for participating in the surfing competition.

Riley stared at the object in amazement. Definitely the coolest surfboard she had ever seen. The colour was a glossy black, as slick as an oil spill, and featured a wild abstract design in splashy purple.

"What do you say we try her out?" C.J. asked.

At first Riley couldn't believe that C.J. actually intended to take this board into the water. It was practically a work of art! "You mean *us*?"

C.J. chuckled. "Who else?" And then he dashed towards the ocean, the board under his arm, his feet kicking up sand.

It was the day after meeting C.J. at the Waverider, and they were already on their first surf date! Riley giggled, zipped up her wet suit, and took off after him, halting at the water's edge.

C.J. was in waist deep, calling her out. "Come on! Nothing to be afraid of!"

Riley took in a deep breath and charged ahead, reaching him in no time flat despite some rocky waves.

C.J. shielded his eyes to study the water from a distance. "There are some monster waves coming down the pike. Ready for a wild ride?"

Riley felt a mixture of fear and excitement. "Are you sure about this?" she asked him. "Remember, I'm just a beginner surfer."

[**Riley**: **Maybe it's because I just watched a surfing competition. Maybe it's the Wheaties I had for breakfast this morning. Or maybe it's because this guy's smile is so fantastic. But suddenly, I am 100% ready to tackle these waves!**]

C.J. gave her a cute cocky grin. "You're with me. You'll be fine."

Riley decided to go for it!

C.J. guided her onto the board and swam beside her as she paddled out to sea. For a while it was rough going, waves breaking, the spray of salt water in her eyes, but with C.J.'s encouragement, she kept after it. Soon she was gliding through the water at a fast clip. In fact, C.J. struggled to keep up with *her*!

"Let's stop here," C.J. said. Though treading now and having just put in a major swim, the Aussie boy was barely breathing hard.

What a hottie! Riley could hardly get over it. With his long blond hair, piercing blue eyes and dark tan, C.J. Logan was movie-star cute.

Suddenly a wild and crazy feeling came over Riley. She had never been out this far in the ocean before. It was scary in a dangerous, fun sort of way. C.J. had started surfing when he was only three years old, so she felt totally safe with him.

"Now it's time for the real fun," C.J. said. He helped Riley straddle the Waverider board, then did the same himself. Together they rode the water, up and down, gathering speed, surfing toward the shore, their legs kicking up a splash.

Riley's stomach did a flip as a major wave lifted them up and swooshed them back down. She screamed in delight. "Wow! That was fun!"

C.J. laughed as they bobbed in the water. "You're good at this. A real natural."

Riley turned back to make eye contact with him. They shared a secret smile. "I want to stand up!" she announced boldly. "I want to surf like you!"

"You asked for it," C.J. said. Within seconds he was standing on the board, the balancing act effortless to him. Then he reached down to take Riley's hands and help her up as well.

After a few stops and starts, she stood steady.

so little time

Just as she established her footing, a serious wave picked them up and they went gliding across the water, zigging and zagging, twisting and turning, until they crashed into the surf.

Riley went under but stayed calm, allowed the rough wave to pass, and surfaced a few moments later. She filled her lungs with oxygen and scanned the area for C.J. She giggled and spun around to see him directly behind her and back on the board. "That was so much fun!"

C.J. extended his hand and helped her up. "Glad you liked it, but we should probably head to shore. The sun will be setting soon, and we shouldn't be in the water at dusk."

They paddled into the shallow end, and Riley felt an alternating sense of exhaustion and elation as her feet hit the wet sand.

"You're great out there," C.J. said.

Riley was proud to get the compliment. "Really?"

"Oh, yeah. A lot of girls won't do anything but lay flat on the board. You're a daredevil."

She couldn't stop smiling. "Well, what can I say? I had a very good teacher."

"I should probably resign though," C.J. said.

Riley didn't understand. "Why?"

"Conflict of interest," C.J. explained. And then he leaned in and kissed her on the cheek.

For a fleeting moment Riley closed her eyes.

C.J.'s lips were soft, and even many seconds after they left her cheek, she could still feel their imprint.

[**Riley: Don't worry, I'm not going to say something cheesy like, "I'll never wash this cheek again!" Although, I must admit, the thought did cross my mind!**]

The rest of the date passed as if part of a dream. They ate chocolate on a blanket, watched the sun begin to set, and swapped stories about parents and school and siblings.

Riley didn't know if she had walked home or floated home. But home she was, holding court in Chloe's room, filling her in on *everything*.

"I can't believe he kissed you!" Chloe squealed.

"It was so sweet and so sudden," Riley gushed. "I was completely shocked." She twirled around the room. "That has to be the best date I'll ever go on in my entire life."

Chloe laughed at her. "Oh, please! How can you say that? You're only fourteen."

"Sometimes a girl just knows," Riley said, a stubborn edge to her voice.

"Listen," Chloe began, "best date of your life or not, I'm happy for you."

Riley smiled. "Thanks."

"At least one of us has a date for Save the Seals," Chloe added.

Riley's smile crashed. "Oh, no!"

"What's wrong?" Chloe asked.

Riley flung herself onto the bed. "I was having so much fun on our date that I forgot to ask him to the dance!"

chapter
eleven

"**I** need Tylenol, several packs of ice, and chocolate-chocolate chip ice cream with rainbow sprinkles."

Chloe and Riley traded worried looks with each other.

"Oh, and the new issues of *Vogue*, *Vanity Fair* and *Women's Wear Daily*." Mom's requests were croaking out of her mouth, each syllable weaker than the last. "Thank you, girls."

Chloe reached for another pillow to elevate Mom's feet. "Even New York's Fashion Week doesn't leave you in this kind of shape."

Mom managed a hint of a smile. "Don't worry, honey. I'll be fine. I have to be. Coach is teaching me how to scuba dive first thing in the morning." There was a yawn, then a groan, and finally the fluttering of eyelids.

[<u>Chloe</u>: **Just between us, I think I'll count to ten before I run around like a crazy person to find everything on Mom's wish list. This baby is going night-night. One thousand one, one thousand two...**]

By the count of one thousand six, Mom was sacked out, snoring, and most likely not to be heard from until the next morning.

Chloe and Riley breathed collective sighs of relief. Now they could see about Dad's dating possibilities, who were scheduled to turn up at his trailer anytime now.

They ran upstairs to grab their clipboards. Then they rushed out to Vista del Mar, a trailer park on a bluff overlooking the beach. It was within walking distance of the house.

A line of women already stood outside Dad's trailer, the smallest one in the whole park.

Chloe approached the group, wondering for a moment if a misunderstanding had occurred. These ladies didn't look anything like their pictures on the Internet.

"Hi, I'm Chloe and this is my sister, Riley. We're going to ask you a few questions for our dad. Think of it as a prescreening interview. After we've talked to everyone, we'll let you know who has been selected to attend the Save the Seals benefit with him, okay?"

Most of the women scowled in response.

A tough-looking lady stepped forward. "Who does this guy think he is – Brad Pitt?"

Chloe glanced at her clipboard. The photograph in this woman's profile must have been taken at least ten years ago. "You must be…"

"Lucy," the woman snapped. "Let's move it along, cookie. I'm already late for a meeting with my probation officer."

Chloe and Riley exchanged concerned glances.

"How are your dancing skills?" Chloe asked.

Lucy grimaced. "Fine. I just stand on a man's feet and tell him to lead."

"Okay, moving on," Chloe said, checking off Lucy's name. "Alexis is next."

A young woman dressed in a bridal gown proceeded to the front of the group. "That's me. FYI, my maid of honour cancelled at the last minute, so I'll need one of you to fill in."

Chloe felt Riley tug on her shirt.

"Uh…this isn't a wedding. It's just about a date for Saturday night," Riley said to the woman.

Chloe referred back to the clipboard and made a note that indicated *not* a match made in heaven.

Alexis ripped off her veil, threw it onto the ground, and began stomping on it. "Why are men so afraid of commitment?" she screamed.

Riley leaned over to whisper in Chloe's ear. "Alexis seems a little high-strung. Dad's more laid back."

Chloe raised her eyebrows. "You think?"

so little time

The remainder of the interviews seemed to go from bad to worse. The best of the lot – a puppeteer named Debbie, whose furry friend, a tiger sock puppet she called Chuckles, never left her side. Yes, she was the normal one of the bunch. The whole exercise had become a least-of-the-ten-evils sort of thing.

Debbie and Chuckles were introduced to Dad, and with great relief Chloe and Riley checked finding him a date off their list of tasks.

Mom was covered, too, provided she woke up from her coma-like sleep in time to get ready for Save the Seals! But the girls had one more person to take care of this Friday night.

They marched back to the house and found Manuelo in the kitchen, fretting over which tie to wear with his best suit.

Chloe and Riley consulted and selected a skinny tie that completed Manuelo's hip look.

"You know, we're getting pretty good at this," Riley said as they headed out of the door for the Newsstand and an evening of speed dating. "We're finding people dates. We're helping them make important fashion choices."

[Chloe: Don't mind my sister. She's still over the moon about C.J. Logan, so her judgment is a little off. I suppose it seems like we're good at it, but at what cost? We're behind on our schoolwork (I've been reading more on-line romance profiles than Shakespeare this week) and behind on our

sleep. (You try getting up before the sun rises to work on Manuelo's love questionnaire!)]

The Newsstand was standing room only with singles hoping to make that special connection. Chloe and Riley practically pushed a nervous Manuelo up to the registration table to sign in. The woman in the FALL IN LOVE FAST — TRY SPEED DATING T-shirt instructed him to have a seat at table number seven.

Chloe and Riley were in luck! They were able to secure a table just off to the side of Manuelo's. From there the girls could see and hear everything that was going on.

"You know, I'm not sure if I'd want to try speed dating," Riley said. "Eight minutes isn't very long to get to know somebody."

Chloe mulled this over. "But what about C.J.? You realised that you liked him in eight *seconds*."

Riley giggled. "This is true."

"Hey, I think it's about to start," Chloe whispered.

Manuelo twisted around and gave them a weak smile.

Chloe gave him the thumbs-up sign. "Just be yourself," she said.

"Yeah," Riley seconded. "You're going to be fine."

But the hour got off to a rough start with Sharon, an efficiency expert who wore her hair in a severe bun that pulled at her face. She never cracked a smile, not even at Manuelo's funniest jokes!

Chloe and Riley had worked out a secret signal with him in advance. If they tugged on their earlobes, it meant DANGER! STAY AWAY. MOVE ON TO THE NEXT ONE.

Greta came next, a female wrestler who towered over Manuelo and probably had a good fifty pounds on him. She was followed by Barbie, an aspiring actress whose energy level dropped off the charts when she found out that Manuelo did not have any Hollywood connections.

"If I pull my ear one more time, it's going to fall off!" Riley said.

Chloe was definitely getting worried now. Manuelo was halfway through and there wasn't even a remote possibility yet.

The second wave of potential dates proved no better. Perhaps the worst of all was Louise, an anger management counsellor who spent her entire eight minutes screaming about a motorist who had cut her off on the freeway.

Each and every time, Chloe and Riley tugged at their earlobes in almost perfect unison. What were they going to do? There was only one more woman left for Manuelo to meet.

But with Melina, their luck took a dramatic turn. She was a chef, too. Not only that, her signature dish was beef Stroganoff! When Manuelo realised that Melina used a hint of fresh nutmeg in her recipe as well, Chloe knew that this was love at first cooking secret!

For the first time all evening, Chloe and Riley

winked at Manuelo. That meant "She's a keeper!"

[Chloe: Okay, you're probably thinking, Wow, this has been one successful night. For about five seconds, I thought so, too. I mean, let's review the facts. Mom is resting. Well, technically she's passed out. Dad is all set up to go out with Debbie. Unfortunately Chuckles will be tagging along, too, but at this point it was a compromise that just had to be made. And Manuelo has found the perfect match. So I should feel amazing, right? Wrong!]

"Houston, we have a problem," Chloe announced. Riley turned to her in alarm. "What now?"

"Reality check," Chloe said gravely. "Everybody has a date for Save the Seals. Everybody but *us*!"

chapter
twelve

Chloe woke up with a start on Saturday morning. An unsettled feeling washed over her. This whole situation with Lennon was truly getting under her skin.

The urge to jump out of bed and write another "Sound Off" burned deep. Only this time *nothing* would be left to interpretation. That's right! Mr. Duh-I-Don't-Get-It would have no trouble understanding her latest article.

As the morning dragged on though, Chloe thought better of it. Enough games already. Why use the school newspaper to tell Lennon what she should be telling him herself? After all, if there was any hope of their dating exclusively, then they were going to have to learn how to talk to each other.

[Chloe: Okay, before you say to yourself, Wow, Chloe is very mature for her age to think about relationships on such a sophisticated level, I should probably come clean on something. I have no intention of listening to anything he has to say. I mean, really. I've been listening to him all week, and he's offered nothing worthwhile. As if he'll suddenly be as verbal as those kids on *Dawson's Creek*. Basically when Lennon answers my phone call later today, he'd better pull up a chair and get comfortable, because I have a lot to say! And after that, I might as well just ask him to the dance. Forget about romance. I need a date!]

The final heat of the Waverider had just begun, and the beach crackled with energy and excitement. Riley felt like a true surfing insider. C.J. had invited her to watch his teammate, Joey B., go for the top title that morning.

As Riley and C.J. watched from the shore with a group of Australian surfers surrounding them, Riley felt a strange sense of conflicting loyalty. A surfer from Malibu was in the running to win, too. In fact, his scores were neck and neck with Joey B.'s.

C.J. nudged Riley. "It's okay if you want your guy to win, mate."

Riley grinned. "Do you call *everybody* 'mate'?"

C.J. grinned back and winked. "Only people I like," he replied.

Suddenly the crowd went crazy.

C.J. whooped and hollered.

The Australian was riding a killer wave, skating

the top of the water like an incredible aqua wonder, leaning in, swaying out. Judging from what Riley could see for herself and the reaction from everyone on the beach, Joey B. would be the man to beat.

When the final scores were announced, C.J.'s teammate had won by a slim margin. Even the hometown crowd screamed their approval and appreciation. It had been a tough competition, and in the end two surfers had given it their all.

C.J. watched as Joey B. engaged in rowdy victory high-fives. "Do you think that'll be me one day?" he asked quietly.

"I have no doubt," Riley said. "Hey, I'd like to treat you to a victory soda at California Dream."

C.J. pretended to be shocked. "This is a total surprise. I was warned that Americans were sore losers," he joked.

Riley playfully shoved the surfer boy who'd had her smiling for the past few days. "Come on. Stop teasing," she laughed.

C.J. got serious all of a sudden. "Maybe I'd like to treat *you* to something."

Riley was intrigued. "Like what?"

C.J. shrugged. "Anything you want. I leave tomorrow, but I'm free tonight."

"Do you like to dance?" Riley asked.

C.J. rocked his body back and forth. "I've got moves you've never seen before."

Riley laughed again. This boy was nothing but

fun! "Then be my date for Save the Seals!" She practically shouted the invitation. "It's a big charity dance. We'll have a great time."

C.J. nodded. "I have no doubt about that," he said. "It's a date."

"Logan, get over here!" a fellow Aussie screamed from down the beach.

Riley and C.J. turned to see the entire Australian surfing team cheering and carrying the big winner on their shoulders.

Almost instantly C.J. broke into a sprint to join them. "You go ahead. I'll catch up in a few minutes," he yelled to Riley.

"See you there!" she called out. Giggling, she watched him join the celebration, then turned and headed for California Dream. To her surprise, she discovered Vance sitting at one of the outdoor tables, looking very bummed out.

"Hey," Riley said. "I never expected to see you here today."

Vance glanced up but didn't offer much. Finally he spoke. "I guess you haven't heard."

"Heard what?" Riley asked.

Vance let out a troubled sigh. "The Tribal Council concert got cancelled."

Riley couldn't believe it. Right away she felt pulled in two directions. She was thrilled about her date with C.J., but now she saw a chance to go with Vance, too. "What happened?"

"The lead singer has nodules on his vocal cords. A doctor here ordered him to take two weeks off." He ran his fingers up and down his soda glass. "I guess I could have gone with you to the Save the Seals benefit dance after all."

For a moment Riley said nothing. Deep down she wished that she hadn't asked C.J. He was a great guy, but he lived in Australia! And Vance was here all the time. "Actually, Vance, I just made plans to go to the dance with someone else."

"Don't worry about it," Vance said. "I'll see you there anyway."

Riley gave him a strange look. "What do you mean? Are you going to the dance?"

"I asked Ariel to go with me," Vance said.

Riley tried to keep her tone in check. "Who's Ariel?" she asked.

"She's the girl who gave my cousin the VIP tickets in the first place. She does street marketing for Tribal Council and goes to Beverly Hills High."

"Oh," Riley mumbled. "How great for her." It was snippy, but Vance didn't seem to notice. She stood there, stunned at the turn of events, trying to sort out her feelings. She should be happy right now. C.J. was amazing, and he was her date for Save the Seals. But something was bugging her big time.

Before Vance asked out Ariel, he didn't know Riley had a date, and the fact that he didn't even bother to find out had her really steamed! As soon as he found out that the concert had been cancelled, she should have been the first person he called. He knew how much she wanted to go to the dance.

Vance stared into his empty soda glass, saying nothing.

I guess all he cares about is the cancelled concert, Riley thought. Not me.

Chloe picked up the phone, dialled Lennon's number, and then put it back down before it started to ring.

Oh, just do it, Chloe. Make the call, she told herself. After a few deep breaths, she did.

Lennon's answering machine clicked on. "Hi, this is Lennon. You're about to hear a beep. I hope you know what to do. If not, you've got serious issues. These things have been around for decades."

Chloe didn't smile at the funny outgoing message. She was too wound up. Finally the signal to begin blasted in her ear. Yikes! She wasn't quite ready. Oh, well. No time like the present.

"Uh, Lennon…hi, this is Chloe. Chloe Carlson. I just wanted to ask you a question. Do you have a problem? Because I think you have a very serious problem. I suggest that you see a doctor about it immediately. By doctor, I mean psychiatrist. Okay. That's all I have to say."

Chloe slammed down the receiver with a bang. Unfortunately she didn't feel better. Plus she forgot to ask him to the dance. Ugh! She hated talking into these things. It made her feel stupid.

But she dialled back anyway, waited for the machine to do its thing, and started in again. "Uh, Lennon, Chloe again. On second thoughts, maybe you don't need to see a doctor. Maybe you need to just look in the mirror and really ask yourself this question: do you actually believe that I'm buying this playing-dumb act of yours? Apparently you didn't get the memo, but I was *not* born yesterday!"

Chloe slammed down the phone again. She felt a little better this time, but, strangely, she had a vague sense of incompleteness. Gosh! She forgot to ask him out *again*. So she dialled Lennon's number once more. This time she would tell him that she had decided to forgive him and then ask him to the Save the Seals benefit dance.

Beep. "It's me again…Chloe. Listen, I'm not quite finished yet. I—"

Chloe heard a click. Someone had picked up the phone. Lennon had been screening her calls and listening to her rants the whole time! She drew in a deep breath. "Lennon?" she asked softly.

"No, this is Shari, Lennon's sister. Please stop stalking my brother."

Chloe gasped. "No, you don't understand. I—"

"You're too young to be so disturbed," the girl said.

"Wait!" Chloe cried. But Lennon's sister had already hung up. Chloe buried her face in her hands. She was mortified. So mortified that there should be a new word for mortified.

chapter
thirteen

Riley managed to get through her soda date with C.J. without appearing upset, then dashed home, determined to vent in her journal about Vance!

When she got there, Tedi was in the living room, standing on a stool, wearing the same animal print dress she was wearing the other day.

"Hi, sweetie," Tedi said with a laugh. "Don't worry. This isn't a time warp. Just my final fitting for the Model of the Year Awards."

Riley smiled. "You look gorgeous."

"Thank you." Tedi beamed. "Believe it or not, models can't hear that enough. Deep down we're all very insecure, you know."

"Where's Mom?" Riley asked.

"She went to apply some more ointment to her wound," Tedi explained.

Riley gasped. "What wound?"

"She snagged a nasty cut on a coral reef while she was scuba diving this morning. It's nothing serious." Tedi gave Riley a big smile. "Hey, how did things go with the boy?"

Riley sighed heavily. "Which one?" she grumbled.

"Sweetie, you're going to have to bring me up to speed," Tedi said.

Riley filled Tedi in on the turn of events with Vance. "I don't know how to feel," she said. "I mean, part of me is mad at him, but another part of me feels kind of silly for being mad."

Tedi mulled over the facts for a moment. "All right, first things first. Never doubt your feelings. They belong to *you*. And if you're having them, then they're valid. End of story."

"Wow," Riley said. "That's really deep, Tedi."

Tedi waved off the praise. "Oh, none of that's mine. I stole it from a self-help book. Don't ask me which one – probably a mixture of several. I love those things. Anyway, this could mean one of two things. One, Vance didn't put you first and you should just forget about him."

Riley's eyes almost welled up in tears. She didn't want to forget about him.

"Or two," Tedi continued, "and this reason is definitely easier to swallow – Vance has too much respect for you to ask at the last minute. I'm sure he probably assumed that you already had a date and didn't want to put himself through that rejection. The ego of a man!" She shook her head. "Sweetie, the stories I could tell you."

That instantly made Riley feel better. Deep down she knew that Tedi's second reason was how Vance was feeling!

Chloe was on a mission to find Lennon. She wanted to apologise for all her crazy messages and explain that she was just disappointed that he didn't get any of her hints to ask her out. The Newsstand was her first stop. It seemed as good a place to start as any, because Lennon loved to hang out there.

She searched the place up and down. No Lennon. Since she was already there, Chloe ordered an iced tea and sat down at a table to decide where to look next. That's when she encountered Nick Wexler, one of Lennon's regular running buddies.

"Hey, Chloe," Nick said. He was parked at a table close to the counter, completely immersed in a hand-held video game. "What's up?"

"Nothing much," she answered, trying to sound very casual. "I thought you'd be hanging out with Lennon today."

"Nah," Nick said, distracted by the video game. "He's out of town for the weekend."

Chloe practically fell out of her chair. "What did you just say?"

Nick shot her an odd glance. "I said he's out of

town. Lennon's got this cool uncle who's an adventure vacation guide. They went on a rafting trip. Lucky guy. I wish *my* uncle did that for a living. Mine manages a Hallmark store in the mall."

At first Chloe couldn't believe what she was hearing, but now everything made perfect sense. Lennon never asked her to the dance because he could never go in the first place!

An enormous wave of relief rolled over her. But it was quickly followed by a wave of dread. Her weird messages were still on Lennon's answering machine. She had to leave another message on his machine, to explain everything!

On second thought Chloe decided against it. She wasn't having much luck with answering machines lately. Especially his.

Instead of writing in her journal, Riley doubled back to California Dream, hoping the whole way that Vance was still there. She had no idea what she was going to say. All she knew was that she wanted to let him know how sorry she was that his big concert plans went bust, and that he would have been her first choice as a date for Save the Seals.

Riley found Vance sitting in the same spot, staring at the same empty soda glass. She felt really bad for him, because she had never seen Vance so disappointed. Obviously, the Tribal Council concert had meant a great deal to him.

"Hey, Vance," Riley said, slipping into the chair next to him. "What's up?"

His mood brightened a little. "What are you doing back here?" he asked.

"I didn't get a chance to say how sorry I was that the concert got cancelled. I know how much you were looking forward to it."

Vance sighed. "I was. But you know, I just need to get over it. There's nothing I can do about it, right? Sulking all day isn't going to change the lead singer's throat problems."

"Did they at least announce a make-up date for the concert?" Riley wondered, hoping to spin his attention on the future.

"Not yet," Vance said. "But when they do, Ariel's promised us tickets."

The pronoun caught Riley off guard. "Us?" she repeated.

"Yeah," Vance said. "She had only one VIP ticket left for this concert, but I told her that next time I definitely needed two. That is, if you want to go with me. Do you?" he asked.

Riley knew that her own eyes were sparkling. "Of course I do!" Maybe Tedi *was* right! Vance liked her so much that he was thinking about her on his worst day. Now she realised that as cute and sweet and fun as C.J. was, Riley really wanted to take Vance to Save the Seals.

Vance reached out for her hand and squeezed

tight. "One more thing. I know you've got a date and everything for Save the Seals tonight, but will you save me a dance?"

"Fast or slow?" Riley asked him. In her heart she wanted a slow dance with Vance.

"A slow dance," Vance said. "Definitely."

chapter
fourteen

The ballroom of the Standard Hotel in Los Angeles was off the hook! The band rocked and the dance floor sizzled.

Chloe moved her hips to the throbbing music. Once again the organisers for Save the Seals had done an awesome job! As it happened, the only person in their household to show up with a date had been Manuelo.

"Look at Manuelo and Melina!" Riley squealed.

Chloe sought them out and finally captured them among the sea of bodies. They were really working it! Those two were incredible on the dance floor.

Chloe and Riley giggled with delight.

For a moment Chloe looked at her sister seriously. "You know, I didn't think you'd be in such a great mood tonight, especially after C.J. had to cancel."

Riley shrugged. "His sponsors had set up a surf clinic that he didn't know about. They paid for his trip here, so he couldn't say no. Besides," she said, shooting a secret glance at Vance across the room, "I don't think a long-distance romance with a boy in Australia is for me, no matter how cute he is!"

"You can say that again!" Chloe cried. Then she beamed a look over to the table where Mom and Dad were sitting. "You know," she said, "they seem to be having a good time just watching everybody."

"Mom couldn't dance if she wanted to," Riley added. "Her feet are too sore from tennis and rock climbing."

"And don't forget about her back," Chloe put in. "It hurts from carrying all that scuba equipment."

"Well," Riley said, "she's better off alone than trying to keep up with Coach Lee. He's way too physical for her."

"Exactly," Chloe agreed. "And I'm so glad that Dad told Debbie that their date was off if she didn't leave Chuckles at home." She observed her parents, who were looking stylish and talking animatedly with another couple. "Yeah," Chloe said, grinning. "Things definitely worked out for the best."

For almost everybody, Chloe thought. After all, she was there with no date and her insane messages were trapped on Lennon's machine. Hopefully, he would get a laugh out of it. She was counting on that.

The pumping dance beat rocked to a finish, and

then the soothing sounds of a love ballad filled the room. Chloe spotted Vance making his way across the crowded dance floor, his eyes locked onto Riley.

"Hey, you promised to save me a dance," he said the moment he reached her.

Riley turned to Chloe, who smiled and gave her sister a thumbs-up. Then Chloe heard a faint buzzing in her beaded Hello Kitty evening bag. It was her mobile phone.

She scooped it out to see a message waiting. From Lennon! He was actually contacting her from his rafting trip. The text read: ARE YOU FREE NEXT WEEKEND?

Chloe smiled as she worked the keypad to craft the perfect response: SATURDAY SOUNDS PERFECT. The girls at school sure did appreciate those words. Hopefully Lennon would as well. Nervously she waited out his response.

IT'S A DATE, he sent back.

Chloe beamed. This game was over. And the best part of all, she and Riley had scored!

mary-kate olsen **ashley** olsen

so little time

Chloe
and Riley's

SCRAPBOOK

so little time

Check out book 10!

a girl's guide to guys

It was Monday afternoon – two more classes to go. Chloe reached into her locker and pulled out a couple of textbooks.

"I checked out the Guide website again over the weekend," she said to Amanda, Tara, and Quinn, who were to waiting to walk down the hall with her. "I can't wait to try the rules out on Lennon."

"I still think you're making a mistake," Amanda said, brushing her hair out of her eyes.

"How can you say that after Friday night?" Tara asked Amanda.

Amanda frowned. "Huh? What happened Friday night?"

"Chloe's very own sister used the Guide on Todd," Quinn explained. "They had a hot date, and now she's acting as if she doesn't like him."

"She *doesn't* like him," Chloe pointed out.

Tara smiled. "That's not what Todd is saying. He said that they made out on the beach. And now Mary-Kate is ignoring him. It's all over school."

Chloe gasped. "What? That totally did *not* happen! What do you mean it's all over—"

Chloe stopped when she saw a girl with short blonde hair rushing out of the girls' bathroom. Her eyes were red, and she had black mascara blotches on her cheeks. She'd obviously been crying.

Quinn sighed. "Poor Adrienne," she whispered.

"Why? What's wrong with her?" Chloe whispered back.

"She met Peter Millis by using the Guide," Tara explained in a low voice. "They were a hot item for a while. Then she stopped following the rules. He broke up with her this weekend – by *e-mail*. Can you believe it?"

Amanda looked doubtful. "That's not what I heard. I heard that Peter Millis just started liking someone else."

"Well, we all know *why*," Quinn said. "Five letters. G-U-I-D-E. Need I say more?"

Wow, the rules in the Guide really *are* powerful, Chloe thought.

Amanda rolled her eyes. "I am so sick of hearing about the Guide! It's so stupid."

"Hey, what about that bet of yours?" Tara asked Amanda. "I thought you were going to prove that the Guide doesn't work."

"Well, Amanda?" Quinn added.

Amanda nodded. "I will. I thought of a plan over the weekend. I'm going to use a rule on some guy I don't know, and he won't even notice that I'm alive. That'll prove once and for all that the Guide doesn't work." She looked up and down the hall nervously. "I – I just have to find a candidate."

Chloe scanned the hall, too. She knew Amanda was shy and would have a hard time getting her experiment going.

Then Chloe spotted *the* guy. "There he is," she said, pointing to a boy across the hall. "Bobby Flynn!"

"Bobby Flynn? Are you crazy, girl?" Tara asked.

Bobby was cute with curly blond hair and blue eyes. So far, he hadn't given Amanda – or any of them, for that matter – the time of day.

"Perfect!" Quinn giggled. "Go for it, Amanda. Try rule number one: 'If you want to meet a guy you're interested in, walk by him slowly and totally ignore him at the same time,'" she recited.

"Wow, you have the rules memorised," Chloe said, impressed.

Amanda regarded Bobby with an apprehensive look. Chloe could tell that she wasn't sure about going through with her plan.

"You can do it," Chloe encouraged her.

Amanda smiled anxiously. "I guess. Okay, here I go. But I'm telling you, I can do rule number one for days and Bobby Flynn isn't going to notice me."

Chloe, Quinn, and Tara stared, mesmerised, as Amanda headed down the hall in Bobby's direction. Just as she was about to pass him, he closed his locker and turned around.

Amanda slowed down – just like the rule said to do – and didn't look at Bobby once.

But Bobby looked at *Amanda*. And looked. And looked.

He couldn't seem to take his eyes off her.

Amanda circled back around to the girls. "See?" she started to say. "The rules don't—"

"Hey, Amanda?"

Chloe saw Bobby rushing down the hall towards them.

"Oh, wow," Tara whispered, elbowing Chloe.

"Hey," Bobby said breathlessly as he stopped in front of Amanda. "Could I talk to you alone for a second? I'm Bobby Flynn. I was wondering if you were doing anything tonight—"

Chloe gasped. She had just seen it with her own eyes. There was no doubt about it. The Girl's Guide to Guys really worked!

mary-kateandashley

TWO of a kind ™

HarperCollins*Entertainment*

PARACHUTE PRESS

DUALSTAR PUBLICATIONS

AOL
mary-kateandashley.com
AOL Keyword: mary-kateandashley

TM & © 2002 Dualstar Entertainment Group, LLC

mary-kateandashley

mary-kateandashley

Sweet 16

(1) *Never Been Kissed*   (0 00 714879 8)
(2) *Wishes and Dreams*   (0 00 714880 1)
(3) *The Perfect Summer*   (0 00 714881 X)

HarperCollins*Entertainment*

PARACHUTE PRESS

DUALSTAR PUBLICATIONS

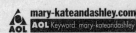
mary-kateandashley.com
AOL Keyword: mary-kateandashley

the **mary-kate**and**ashley** brand

Fab freebies!

You can have loads of fun with these ultra-cool Glistening Stix from the **mary-kate**and**ashley** brand. Great glam looks for eyes, lips – or anywhere else you fancy!

All you have to do is **collect four tokens from four different books from the mary-kate**and**ashley brand**

(no photocopies, please!), send them to us with your address

Go on, get collecting and sparkle like a star!

Name: ....

Address: ....

....

e-mail: ....

☐ Tick here if you do not wish to receive further information about children's books.